IE MAN FROM PAINTED ROCK

For   a year, the Up and Down ranch has been
plag   by a series of thefts, mainly cattle; but now
the   man, Hard Ross, has lost the mare he raised
fron   illy. Then a new owner rolls up to the ranch
in h   red automobile: "Fancy" Jim Sherrod, a city
guy   d first-class dandy — and instant laughing
stock f the cowhands. Hard Ross isn't amused,
how   r, and decks his new boss as soon as he
rece   an order demeaning to his respected
posi   . He's headed for the road — until Sherrod
strik   deal with him: stay for a month and help
him   the ranch until he can get the swing of it.
But   re's more to Fancy Jim Sherrod than meets
the   — as cowhands and rustlers alike will soon
disc   , when the bullets start to fly . . .

SPECIAL MESSAGE TO READERS

THE MAN FROM PAINTED ROCK

JACKSON GREGORY

SAGEBRUSH
Large Print Westerns

First published in Great Britain by Collins
First published in the United States by Dodd, Mead

First Isis Edition
published 2019
by arrangement with
Golden West Literary Agency

The moral right of the author has been asserted

A catalogue record for this book is available
from the British Library.

ISBN 978-1-78541-688-0 (pb)

Published by
F. A. Thorpe (Publishing)
Anstey, Leicestershire

Set by Words & Graphics Ltd.
Anstey, Leicestershire
Printed and bound in Great Britain by
T. J. International Ltd., Padstow, Cornwall

This book is printed on acid-free paper

CHAPTER
ONE

When "Hard" Ross was mad he wasn't a pretty thing to look upon. His rage surged upward through his sunburned cheeks and flared like fire into his grey-blue eyes that were usually cool. The men who went to him for orders and pay, and in whose strong hands the destinies of the Up and Down Cattle Range had resided for a matter of years, were not afraid of him, since they were not the sort of men to be afraid of anything that walked or had a name in the dictionary. But they had a way, at times like this, of going very quietly about their business.

"Do about it!" bellowed Hard Ross at the half-dozen quiet men in the bunkhouse. "What am I going to do about it, huh? Go to the law, you say, Harper? Yes, I'll go to the law, by God! The law that men have gone to ever since Adam, a long time before the time of crooked sheriffs and rotten judges! The old law, the law there ain't no bribing an' no buying up, the law of a man's right hand!"

It was a long speech for Hard Ross to make before breakfast, a rare bit of eloquence from him at any time, and the men looked at him curiously. Even Sunny

Harper, whose yellow, tousled hair and eternal grin gave him his name, condescended to be serious.

"What's happened recent?" he asked. "Everything was all right when we hit the hay last night."

"All right?" cried Hard Ross angrily. "You mean we thought it was. Is it all right if a man goes to sleep with a rattler in his blankets or a skunk under his pillow, just because he don't know he's got that kind of company? It wasn't all right any more'n it's been off an' on for a year now. Only this time I got something I can put my hands on!"

There was something interesting, almost tangible in the storm of the foreman's anger. The men, to the last man of them, looked at him with sharp and expectant eyes.

"It's Silver Slippers this time!" Hard Ross flung the statement at them as he might have hurled a missile at the head of a man he hated. "She's gone!"

"Silver Slippers?" queried Little John Sperry, his voice a weak, incredulous gasp. "Why, I tied her in her stall last night, Ross. I watered her an' fed her the last thing."

"An' she's clean gone this morning," snapped Hard Ross.

"Maybe she broke away an' —" began Little John a bit uncertainly.

"Maybe I'm a fool, huh?" Ross cut him short. "Maybe she shut the barn door after she went out, after I dropped the bolt in the staple, huh? There's no maybe about it; she's been stole the same as one hell of a lot of other things has been stole during less'n a year. An' this

2

time I got both eyes open, an' I'm getting the deadwood on the man I want! You boys just set still an' watch an' you'll see something."

They sat still, all but Hard Ross, who stood at the open door, and the cook, who remained by his stove, a black stream of steaming liquid escaping from the coffee-pot in his hands and spattering upon the rough boards of the floor. And then another man came in, a big fellow with round, muscular shoulders and smouldering eyes.

He came to the door from the well, where he had been washing, glanced carelessly about the long, low room, saw Hard Ross and the bright, hard anger in Hard Ross's eyes, and started back. Every movement this man made was quick, but his leap now, sideways and back, was not quick enough. Hard Ross's big hands had flashed outward, they had settled upon the other man's shoulders, they had jerked him off his feet and into the room and slammed him back, all in a second, so that his shoulders struck heavily against the wall.

"Hawley," said the foreman, his voice quiet now, his eyes alight with a perfect joy of rage, "I'm goin' to give you the beating of your life!"

"What's the matter?" cried Hawley, his big hands wrenching at the other man's wrists. "What's eating you, Ross? Just because you happen to be boss here, you ain't going —"

For answer Hard Ross jerked his right hand free, and with his hard muscles cording to the effort, drove it straight from the shoulder into Hawley's face.

Hawley's head snapped back, striking the wall, and he swayed a moment, all but stunned from the one blow; then with a powerful effort he wrenched away from the one hand holding him and sprang to one side. As he leaped the blood was running across a cut cheek and cut lips; his face was distorted with a wrath no less than Ross's; his hand flew to his hip pocket.

"You damn fool!" he gasped chokingly. "I'll kill you for that!"

But Hard Ross was not a fool, and he had no wish for pistol play this morning. He, too, leaped forward. He struck again before Hawley's hand could make the short journey to bulging hip pocket, and there was no man there in the bunkhouse who could have taken that second blow square in the face and stood up under it.

Hawley did not reel now; he fell heavily, not partially stunned but stunned entirely; and where he fell he lay very still.

Suddenly it was very quiet in the bunkhouse. The cook remembered his dribbling coffee-pot and placed it back upon the stove. The men who had pushed back their chairs from the breakfast table came forward, looking at the man on the floor.

"You mean he done it?" queried Sunny Harper gently.

"I've just explained what I mean in words a young baby might understand," grunted Ross. He stooped, jerked the revolver from Hawley's pocket, and flung it under one of the bunks. "Give him some water, cookie. Out'n the bucket."

4

But it was Sunny Harper who brought a bucketful of cold water from the well and splashed it over the unconscious man's face and wrists. In a little while Hawley opened his eyes, wiped the blood from his face, and sat up. And as he moved his body, he moved his right hand. It went swiftly to his hip, found an empty pocket, and dropped again to the floor.

"What's the next play?" he asked coolly. His eyes, hard, sharp, malevolent, were upon the foreman's. "I'm down an' out, I guess, seeing as how you took me when I wasn't looking."

"I just naturally took you as soon as I could get you," grunted Ross. "I couldn't wait, that's all."

"An' now maybe you're going to tell me what you done it for?" he said with a keen questioning look in his smouldering eyes.

"No, I ain't. Seeing as you know as well as I do! But I'm going to tell the other boys, an' there ain't no objection to you listening. You boys know how I put this Hawley on the pay list more'n a month ago. You know we didn't need an extra man real bad, an' you wondered why I done it, I reckon? I put him on because I had the hunch he was a crook, that's why!

"There's another man we've all got our eyes on quite a spell now, an' that's Bull Plummer of the Bar Diamond outfit. Well, I'd seen this man Hawley with Plummer, chummy as two of a kind, last time there was races in town, an' I made the bet when he showed up for a job that Plummer was back of it, an' that means something crooked. So I put him on an' watched him.

5

"During the last two months there ain't been any cattle lost, but I figgered he was just getting solid with us first. An' then, last night, he couldn't stand it any longer. I heard him come back into the bunkhouse about two o'clock, an' I hadn't heard him go out. But now it's plain as print to me that he's the gent who stole the finest blooded little mare as ever was foaled this side the Rockies. An' any man as lays a hand on Silver Slippers gets what Hawley just got."

Hawley, sneering, drew himself up and stood against the wall.

"What do you think I done with her?" he demanded. "I went outside to get a drink, an' was gone about ten minutes. Think I et her?"

Ross shook his head.

"I don't know what's gone with her," he replied bluntly. "She's gone, and you know what went with her. I reckon you put up the job with Plummer, an' he rode over or sent one of his yellow crowd to take her off your hands."

The smile which came and lingered upon Hawley's cut lips was not pretty.

"You're sure great at guessing things," he said slowly. "Only you're quite some ways off in your guesswork, Mr. Ross. An' as for proof —"

"Proof!" snorted Ross, flaring up again. "Do you take me for the sort of man that's going to wait for proof? I know you're a damn crook, an' I know you had a hand in the taking of Silver Slippers, just as you've had a hand in a whole lot of Bull Plummer's rotten play right along. That's enough for me, Hawley. Now, listen to this: Do you want to know why I just beat you up a little instead of killing you outright as you deserve?"

"I ain't curious," muttered Hawley.

"All right. But then maybe the rest of the boys has got a right to know why I'm being so gentle with you after you've laid your dirty paws on the finest little mare as ever slapped her feet down on a cow range. An' I'm telling 'em so's you can hear if you want to! Boys," and his deep voice went husky with the new emotion in it, "you know I'm putting it straight when I say that there never was a mare that could make Silver Slippers eat her dust. An' what I'm going to say maybe sounds mushy, but I don't care a single damn what it sounds like. It's so, an' I ain't the man to shy at the truth."

And yet he did shy a little and hesitated and cleared his throat before he went on.

"It sounds funny, coming from a man like me," the foreman continued, shifting a bit uneasily under many watchful eyes. "But I reckon there is just one thing in the world as counts. An' it's love! Now wait a minute," he exploded with sudden fierceness, "until I can finish what I've begun, or I'll have to beat somebody else up this morning. It's love I'm saying, an' that's about what I'm meaning. There's diff'rent kinds of love. I ain't ever loved a woman an' I ain't going to. I ain't ever been mad in love with whisky nor with poker. I don't know as a man can say I've been crazy mad in love with life even. But Silver Slippers — my God! I raised her from a sucking filly, an' I broke her, an' no man but me has ever slapped a leg across her back. Now you know what I mean?"

For a brief, uncertain moment the man's hard eyes were unbelievably soft, and more than one man there, wondering, saw that they were wet. And then suddenly swinging about upon Hawley so that he shrank back from what he saw in eyes no longer soft or wet, Hard Ross cried harshly:

"Why didn't I pound the last spark of life out'n you? Why? Just because I want that little mare back! Just because you're the one man I know who can go get her for me. An' I'm passing it to you straight, Hawley, if you waste any time putting Silver Slippers back there in the barn, without a scratch on the silk of her hide, why then, so help me, I'm goin' to kill you!"

Hard Ross's jaws shut with a little click of the large, strong teeth. He turned abruptly and went to the breakfast table. The other men, silent for a little while, went to their chairs. Hawley, his face dead-white save for the scarlet threads of blood across it, turned and went down to the corral for his horse.

And then a stranger came into camp and everything was forgotten in the shock of his coming.

CHAPTER
TWO

It is a saying in the West that the law and barb-wire fences travel together; that one is as treacherous as the other; and that when they both come, the cattle country has got to move on.

The law and barb-wire fences had not yet invaded the mountain valleys in the Up and Down country. Sheriffs were not unheard of, but the district was big and wild and eminently self-dependent, and men had not forgotten the world-old way of settling their own arguments with their hands.

The Up and Down had been having its troubles for upward of a year now. Trouble upon the range is likely to mean just one thing: the loss of cattle for one reason or another. And, where fences and law have not come, the loss is very likely explained by the one word, "rustlers." For, wherever there are men there are strong men and weak, good men and bad, and wherever there are cattle and the opportunity, there are men to seek the short-cut to gold or the gallows.

When the Creation piled the high masses of the mountains and carved the deep-sided valleys, the opportunity was made. The Up and Down range had its natural boundaries, defined since Time was young.

There was the valley, twenty miles of it in length, so narrow here and there that a cowboy riding upon one edge under the cliffs might pick off with his Winchester a deer browsing upon the far side, bulging in places to a width of half a dozen miles. It was the Valley of the Twin Lakes.

At the "Upper End," the creek which carried away the surplus of the two little lakes' clear water to wander westward through the valley, had its beginning under tall sheer cliffs in a white froth over echoing waterfalls. For a man to climb the cliffs there on foot was a day's work; for him to climb them on horseback was an impossibility. There was one of the range's Nature-made fences.

Upon the two sides of the valley, north and south, the mountains stood steep in roughly parallel lines extending almost to the "Lower End," twenty miles away. There were places here and there, narrow, rocky defiles rather than true passes, through which it was possible for cattle to work their way out and up, across the uplands, and so over into a neighbouring range. But out of the score of men taking their pay from Hard Ross, foreman, there were always men whose allotted duty it was to visit these gorges daily, to see that there were no restless steers seeking to leave the home range, to examine the ground for the tracks which would tell if even a calf had gone that way.

And still, with all precautions the foreman took, again and again during the year cattle had been lost. They were gone from the range, and no close night-herding had been able to lessen the losses. A dozen big steers had gone in one herd, and that when big steers were worth seventy dollars a head. They hadn't gone away of their own will, they hadn't gone through the rocky passes, that much Hard Ross knew. But that was all that he did know about it. They were gone, eight hundred dollars gone in a night. And picked cattle they were too. The man who had engineered their theft had gone about his business coolly. He had picked and chosen; he had defied vigilance; he had laughed at precautions.

And that was not all. Again and again, a single steer, or three or four beef cattle, "turned up missing."

It was Bull Plummer's work. That was the one thing of which Hard Ross was growing more and more positive. For, certainly, of all the men none had a better opportunity than Bull Plummer to do this sort of thing, and no man had a harder reputation.

Plummer was owner and his own foreman of the Bar Diamond outfit, and the Bar Diamond lay parallel to the Up and Down just across the ridge to the west. If once Plummer and the hard crowd taking their wages from him could get the cattle across the ridge and into Bar Diamond territory, the rest would be simple enough. From there it was only a night's drive to the railroad; and, to the cattlemen, railroad and crooked business were synonymous.

Such were conditions upon the morning when Hard Ross lost a mare five hundred dollars could not have bought, lost his temper, and bruised his fist upon the face of Hawley, the new man.

"Anyway," muttered Ross as he watched the men going down to the corrals for their horses, "one good thing, I don't have to report this to the Old Man down in the city. It's my loss, an' it ain't his. An' I'm sick and tired making reports how more stock is lost."

He didn't know yet what he was going to know in five minutes: he had made his last report to the owner in the city.

He went back into the bunkhouse, took up his hat and tobacco, and turned again to the door. Then it was that he saw the stranger coming into camp.

He was a strange sort of stranger, his way of coming stranger still; and big Ross grunted his disgust. The road into the valley from the nearest town, White Rock, thirty miles away, was as poor a road as a man ever strove manfully to engineer a Studebaker wagon along. And yet, coming up over a knoll in the floor of the valley was a big red touring car.

The automobile's engine was resting; the propelling power was a team of mules; the car rocked and jolted along behind a heavy log chain; a man riding on horseback at the side of the mules handled the reins and the necessary flow of language; and another man, the stranger, sat smiling upon the seat of his car and gazing with mild eyes upon the landscape through a pair of nose spectacles.

"A city guy coming camping," grunted Hard Ross, jamming his hat hard down over his brows. "He'll be shooting at deer an' killing my cattle for me."

12

Then the mules came down the knoll at a swinging trot, the driver jerked them to a standstill in front of the bunkhouse, and the man in the car smiled pleasantly upon Hard Ross and wished him an amiable good morning. The boys at the corrals saw, saddled swiftly, and rode back to the bunkhouse to gaze upon the newcomer.

The newcomer smiled upon them all and got down. He had all the earmarks of a city guy, all right. In the first place, he wore a stiff hat, a derby. Then, he wore nose-glasses. Then, he was dressed in patent ties, in a neatly tailored and pressed grey suit, in new tan gloves. A fishing rod, newly bought in White Rock, thrust its way upward like a mast; a rifle in a brand-new case stood in the corner of the tonneau; there were suitcases and travelling bags innumerable. These things the cowboys saw before they saw the man himself.

Then the man under the clothes. He looked insignificant as he sat in his automobile; but on the ground, standing upon legs from which he strove to drive the cramp and stiffness, it appeared that he was a tall, rangy, not ungraceful young fellow of perhaps twenty-five or thirty, who might have posed nicely for the pictures of Kuttenheimers' Swell Suits which decorated the signboards just outside of White Rock.

One hand came out of its tan glove and showed soft and white. There was a smudge of ink upon the thumb and forefinger which Ross was quick to see and which caused another disgusted grunt.

He was close-shaven, had shaved last night. He wore a gaily coloured vest, a high white collar of the latest fashion, just like the collar the dudes in the Kuttenheimer Swell Suits pictures wore, a tie of blue birdblue, a diamond stickpin. His eyes were a soft brown, filled with much mild curiosity as they ranged from Hard Ross to the rest of the boys.

"Which one of you men is Mr. Ross?" he asked when nothing but stares and still tongues greeted his arrival.

"I am," answered Ross shortly. "What do you want?"

The young man offered his hand and his name together.

"I'm Mr. Sherrod." He added a smile to the two other offerings. "I've come to stay with you a while."

There was no glad hospitality in Hard Ross's sniff. He had troubles enough already. But the young man ran on quickly, drawing back his hand from the clutch Ross had been pleased to give him and wiping it upon a white linen handkerchief.

"I've brought you a letter from Mr. Hodges." He felt in his pockets, seemed alarmed, muttered, "Mercy! I'm afraid I've lost it — No," he concluded, with his beaming smile coming back, "here it is." He handed it to the foreman.

Ross took it swiftly, a little angrily, his sole thought that this young whipper snapper was some friend of Mr. Hodges, the owner of the Up and Down, and that the letter was asking Ross to make his stay a pleasant one, to have one of the boys show him where the best trout-fishing was to be found, to point out the likely places for deer, to watch over him so that he didn't fall off a cliff somewhere or take a drop into one of the little lakes and drown. But what Hard Ross read was this:

DEAR ROSS:

This will inform you that I have sold the Up and Down, brand and all, to Mr. Sherrod, to whom this will introduce you.

D. M. HODGES.

Hard Ross's comment was brief, characteristic, and perhaps all that could be expected. He looked from the letter in his hand to the touring car, to the man who had handed it to him, and said softly, "Well, I'll be damned!"

One would have said that young Mr. Sherrod's smile was of the brand warranted not to come off. He lifted his eyebrows, adjusted his glasses, and beamed.

"Something of a surprise, eh?" he chuckled. "Well, well, so it is to me, too, my good fellow. But I had a pile of money, you know, and I was deuced well tired of the usual thing, you know, so I thought I'd have a try at it. Say, it's great out here, isn't it? And all this is mine now? This whole valley, those cows over yonder, the cliffs, the view and all? I'm going to have the time of my life! I say, Ross, give this other fellow a hand with my traps, there's a good fellow. I dare say the cook's got some coffee and biscuits and eggs? I'll run in and have a mouthful. I rode all night." He beamed over his shoulder, as he turned to the bunkhouse door. "I wanted to get here before the men went to work. You men wait until I come out. You take your orders from me now, you know."

For a moment there was silence as Mr. Sherrod disappeared in search of breakfast. Then, simultaneously, there came a stifled curse from Hard Ross and a burst of laughter from the men upon their horses, a peal of merriment in which Sunny Harper's musical baritone led in a paroxysm of pure glee.

A cowpunch isn't afraid of work, and does many things during the day which soil his hands. He doesn't mind that. But if there is a thing he abhors more than he does a sheep-herder, it is the type of human, called man for want of a proper name, who dances around at the behest of the idle rich, doing petty, servile things which the idle rich should do for himself.

The other men laughed, Hard Ross swore again and with deeper, fuller meaning, and Mr. Sherrod's things stayed in the automobile.

"As if it wasn't bad enough already!" bellowed the foreman. "An' now a man like him comes an' is going to give his own orders, an' the Up and Down is going to eternal hell in a handbasket!"

"Look out, Ross," grinned Little John. "He'll hear you, an' you'll get yourself fired. He don't need a foreman, anyhow. Shucks, he can run a little outfit like this single-handed!"

"An' I don't want the job of keeper for a crazy man or mama for a mollycoddle," snorted Ross. "Let him fire me and be damned."

But the coming of the man, fashionable clothes, inconsequential air, city manner and all, had had their sobering effect. The men, about to begin the day's work, were suddenly stopped and must await the work he chose to give them. For he was the owner; and after all, though they had lived on the range long before he

16

had heard of it, though it was home to them, they were hired men who had to obey his orders — or quit.

Evidently Mr. Sherrod was hungry and had little thought for the idle men waiting for him. It was close to half an hour before he came out to them, carefully lighting a huge black cigar.

He was evidently in a contented frame of mind. The line of his chest showed prominently under the gay-coloured vest, his eyes were filled with smiling satisfaction as once more they swept the faces about him and went on to the steep walls of the valley. Then he seemed to remember the first and only order he had been pleased to give, saw his baggage still where he had left it, and turned, frowning, to Ross.

"I say," he called sharply. "I said you were to take those things into the house for me. Didn't you hear me?"

"I sure enough heard you," was Ross's surly answer. "I been holding down my job quite some time as puncher first an' foreman next, but I'm double-damned if I ever agreed to take on the sort of jobs made for a boot-licking valet. If you want that stuff moved, I reckon the best way is to get in an' move it yourself."

There was a note of finality in Hard Ross's tone. The day had begun badly for him, the spirit within him was still sore and chafed, the early morning anger was not yet entirely cooled. Else it is possible that he might have grinned and taken the new owner's orders. But the spirit of revolt was high in him now, and there was no man who walked from whom Hard Ross was in the mood to take such orders as these.

Mr. Sherrod's eyes showed a vast amazement. He pushed his derby far back upon his head, adjusted his glasses, and stared. His expression was that of a tourist in a far land being showed one of the wonders of the world.

"You mean," he said slowly, as if he groped in the dark of a stupefied brain for each word, "that you refuse to do what I tell you to do?"

Any answer was so very unnecessary that Hard Ross made none. He stared back, his contempt leaping high in his eyes. Sunny Harper giggled like a girl in her teens, and then grew suddenly and gravely interested in the loose leather about his saddle-horn.

"I'd have you understand," said Mr. Sherrod with dignity, "that this range is mine. It's been mine for a month. You've been drawing pay from me. And if my servants won't do what I tell them —"

"Servants!" boomed Hard Ross, his face red, his big hands twitching. "Servants, you little hop-o'-my-thumb! Why, you say that to me again and I'll slap your face for you!"

A little thing, perhaps, this slip of the tongue of Mr. Sherrod's.

But then, to a man like Hard Ross and upon a day like to-day, it was like a goad.

"Mercy!" gasped the new owner of the Up and Down. "You — you impudent boor! I — I — if you so much as laid a hand on me, I'd have you arrested and sent to prison for six months! I — I've a notion to have you arrested, anyway. Mr. Hodges has told me how his

18

cattle, my cattle now, have been stolen! I thought it looked funny."

"Hold on!" shouted Hard Ross angrily. "You go easy, little cock-o'-the-walk. You just hint I ain't straight —"

"I believe you're what you look like," fumed Mr. Sherrod. He drew a step backward and spat out: "You act like a cattle-thief, you look like a cat —"

Whether his meaning ended there, whether he sought to affirm that he had discovered something feline in the glare in Hard Ross's eyes, or whether he was going to explain that the man looked like a rustler, was not made plain.

Hard Ross's nerves were tingling. Hard Ross's hand was twitching again. He struck — Mr. Sherrod had not stepped far enough back — his open palm smote heavily upon the freshly shaven cheek; and the new owner of the Up and Down measured the length of his immaculate suit upon the dust by the bunkhouse door.

CHAPTER
THREE

"You little weak-eyed rabbit!" choked Hard Ross, as he stood over the form stretched upon the ground, both big fists doubled now with knuckles fast growing white. "I've stood about all my constitution's good for since sunup. You get up an' you apologize, or by all that's holy, I'll slap the white face clean off'n you!"

This from man to master! This from a hired cowhand to a man who must be close to a millionaire to purchase an outfit like the Up and Down! Mr. Sherrod gazed at him as if stupefied, and made no attempt to get to his feet. He moved a little, found the glasses at his side, held them up to his nose, and stared up into the flushed face above him.

From it he stared at the circle of other faces. And when he had seen only rage on the one distorted countenance, amused contempt on the others, he fumbled with his glasses, dropped them, and said querulously:

"I say, Ross, this is no way to cut up, you know. I — I may have been mistaken. I — well, I was a trifle angry, I suppose. No doubt you are honest enough."

Ross turned his back square upon the owner of the Up and Down.

"You boys don't take any more orders off'n me," he said quietly. "It's up to you an' this city guy."

And he strode back to the bunkhouse, slammed the door after him, and went to throwing into a barley sack what few of his personal effects he would take with him when he rode out looking for a new job.

Mr. Sherrod looked after the rude departure with uplifted eyebrows, and then got slowly to his feet, one hand laid upon the cheek which Hard Ross had struck, the other beating the dust out of his trousers and coat.

"I call you men to witness that the assault was unprovoked," he said sharply. "Now, go about your work. Do whatever that man had told you to do for the day. I — I'm a trifle upset. Any man with any sort of sensibilities would be. Merciful goodness! — I'll give you your orders to-morrow."

They went, went in a whirlwind of dust and gleeful laughter, seeking as much to hide the one as the other. And Mr. Sherrod took a step toward the bunkhouse door, stopped, rubbed his chin reflectively, and finally threw the door open.

"You're going to quit?" he demanded, his foot on the threshold.

"No," snapped Ross. "I've quit already."

"Is — is it necessary," Sherrod said hesitatingly, "for you to go this way, without any warning?"

"For the love of God!" cried Hard Ross wonderingly. "Do you want me to knock you down first and then keep on working for you?"

"Why, I don't want you to knock me down at all. I never wanted that. But I say, a man ought to be reasonable. I want you to stay a day or so and sort of look after things until I can get my hand in. Oh," he put in hurriedly, "no doubt the work is easy enough and simple. But then for a man to pitch right in, his first day on a cow ranch, and run it — Come now. Be a good fellow, Ross. I made a mistake, and we'll forget it. I want you to stay."

Hard Ross put down his sack, went to a bunk, sat down and sought for paper and tobacco.

"I don't quite get you, stranger," he said heavily. "I just knocked you as flat as a doormat, didn't I? An' now you're asking me to forget an' stick on the job? Say, what are you giving me?"

"I'm giving you seventy-five dollars a month and board and room," the new owner answered quickly. "And I tell you I want you to run this ranch for me until I can get the swing of it. It may take me a month, I don't know how long."

"A month!" gasped Hard Ross. He forgot to roll into a cigarette the tobacco he had poured into his paper. "You learn to run a cow outfit in a month!"

"Well, well," said Sherrod quickly. "I'll do my best. And, say, you'll stay won't you? There's a good fellow."

Ross looked at him with open, unconcealed contempt. But Hard Ross was thinking. Jobs like this were not plentiful. If he gave this one up, he might be months getting anything better than the poor wages the rest of the boys drew. Then there was Bull Plummer still to settle with, and there was Hawley — and Silver Slippers. Somehow it galled him to keep his place under a man like Sherrod. And yet . . .

"It's your range, Mr. Sherrod." He shrugged his heavy shoulders. "If you want me to stay, why, I'll stay."

"Then it's settled," Mr. Sherrod sighed and came on into the room.

He found a chair, disposed his tall frame in it languidly, brought a fresh cigar from his vest pocket, saw through his nose-glasses that the fine Sumatra wrapper had come to grief in his recent violent meeting with his tempestuous foreman, tossed it away, selected another, lighted it very carefully, and surveyed Hard Ross through the upcurling smoke.

"I want a word or two with you before the day's work begins."

"Fire ahead," muttered Hard Ross.

"I've brought an outfit along with me," said Mr. Sherrod with dignity. "I got it in the city, and the man who sold it to me told me that it was just a little bit of all right. Now, I'm in for this game, Ross, and I'm going to start to-day. First thing, I want you to look over my things and pass on them. Will you do it?"

Ross grumbled out a curt, "Sure." Mr. Sherrod seemed upon the point of giving an order, hesitated, and rising swiftly went out to his touring car. From his pile of baggage he brought forth a neat black bag which with his own white hands he lugged into the bunkhouse. From the bag he brought forth articles which caused Hard Ross to gasp with astonished amusement.

There were all the "trimmings" of a theatrical cowpuncher. A brand-new Stetson with an enormously wide soft brim, a scarlet neck-scarf, a bright blue silk shirt, a pair of black boots with monstrously high heels, a pair of spotlessly white chaps, a bridle with Spanish bit whose silver chasings flashed gaily in the morning sunlight. And — Hard Ross drew in a deep, lung-filling breath and nearly choked on it — there was a broad cartridge belt with two heavy-calibre Colt revolvers swinging from it. The cook, upon the verge of stifling and mindful of keeping the best job he had ever had, went hurriedly outside for a bucket of water.

"Are they all right?" queried Mr. Sherrod, his gaze as full of anxiety as a child's as he laid one article after the other upon the table.

"They're sure all right!" answered Hard Ross.

"And — I haven't forgotten anything, have I?" Mr. Sherrod asked even more anxiously.

"Good Lord, no!" burst fervently from Hard Ross. "You haven't missed a bet!"

Mr. Sherrod's sigh bespoke a vast satisfaction. He smiled upon his foreman with returning amiability.

"I say, Ross," he said eagerly, "I don't doubt that we're going to forget all about our little misunderstanding of this morning, aren't we? I dare say we're going to be real friends when we get to understand each other. Now, I've come out here to go to work with my sleeves rolled up, to speak figuratively. I haven't brought any foolish notions along with me. I'm willing to forget the difference in our stations and consider that we're just men and equals on the job. That's fair, now, isn't it?"

"That's fair," returned Ross, his head down now, his big fingers very busy with his cigarette-building.

24

"I'm going to show you that I mean business." Mr. Sherrod was divesting himself of his outer clothing as he spoke, and began to don hastily the gay regalia of the Behind-the-Footlights cowboy costume. "I'm going out to ride over the ranch with you this morning." He jerked on his snow-white chaps and buckled his belt about his waist, a heavy revolver swinging in its new holster at each hip. "The first thing will be a horse. Say, Ross, is there an extra saddle-animal on the ranch that — er — that is full of life and all that and yet that — er — that a man can trust? That won't go to bucking, you know?"

Hard Ross's first thought had dallied with the temptation of giving this man the worst horse of the outfit. Now he felt ashamed of himself.

"The pore devil's trying to be a man, anyhow," he told himself thoughtfully. "He's trying to be fair." And he decided to pick out one of the older, quieter horses for his new boss.

"There's just one more thing, and we can go to work." Mr. Sherrod paused, saw that the cook had gone down to an outhouse for something, and went on swiftly, "I guess I did make a mistake this morning, Ross. I want you to forget it. Will you — Do you ever drink anything?"

"I ain't never missed the chance," grinned Ross. "Not since I was ten."

"Just after breakfast — you don't mind that?"

"There's just three times a man ought to drink licker," Ross informed him gravely. "One is before meals, one is during meals, an' the other is between meals. Don't wait on me."

Mr. Sherrod laughed, seemed again upon the verge of giving an order, thought better of it, and went back to the automobile. He brought out a large suitcase this time, lugged it into the bunkhouse, closed the door, and opened the suitcase.

From the suitcase came a bottle, and there was scarcely a flicker of surprise in Hard Ross's steady eyes when he saw that the thing he was called upon to drink to forgetfulness of an insult and to a better understanding, was champagne. The bottle popped, and they drank from two thick earthen coffee cups. And when they had done, Hard Ross, a little apologetically, asked:

"You haven't got any whisky along, have you? Just to wash the taste out with?"

Then they had whisky together. And then, side by side, they went down to the corral, Mr. Sherrod in glittering new spurs, boots, chaps, and nose-glasses. When the proper horses were lassoed by Ross's unerring rope, a gentle old mare for the new owner, a wild, untamed brute of a four-year-old for the foreman, they rode away together across the rolling floor of the valley. And when, an hour later, they met a couple of the boys cutting out a herd of calves at the north corrals, Hard Ross, being a gentleman in the uncouth heart of him, looked straight and steadily ahead and gave no sign of having seen the drooping eyelids and keen delight upon the faces which greeted the spectacular appearance of Mr. Sherrod, owner of the Up and Down cattle outfit.

CHAPTER
FOUR

To a man of inquiring mind, there should be no more interesting study than the mysterious radiation of news from any given point in the cattle country to a thousand little nooks and corners where telegraphs and telephones and daily newspapers are unknown. It is as if it were borne upon the chance wind, carried with the flood of a gossiping creek, sung across the wide spaces by the whispering tongues of pine-needles, dropped here and yonder like rain from the bursting bosoms of scudding clouds.

Within two days from the time of the coming of the new owner to the Up and Down, word of the event had gone its thirty-mile way to White Rock and from that bustling outpost upon the skirts of the casually cultivated lands had run its many ways over the lower valley country. Within five days White Rock had distorted, magnified and transmitted the tale to the utmost of its wonderful ability.

Within ten days it is to be doubted if there was a man, woman or child anywhere within a radius of fifty miles who had not heard of the theft of Silver Slippers, the punishment meted out to Hawley, the coming of Sherrod, and his reception by his foreman. The delicate morsel upon the tongue of gossip was the characterisation of Sherrod himself, and gossip went womanfully to her task.

Then, after the news went up and down in many directions and to great distances, it travelled across the South Ridge upon the border of the Up and Down and dropped down into the corrals of Bull Plummer, foreman and owner of the Bar Diamond. And Bull Plummer, being a man of resource and initiative, got busy.

Mr. Sherrod had been with his outfit for two weeks, during which time he had had many adventures, though he had not fallen over the edge of a cliff, got himself drowned in the lakes, or had his head kicked off by a vicious horse in the corrals. He had fired one of his heavy revolvers in the general direction of a coyote, to the boundless glee of the two men who happened to be with him, Sunny Harper and a man they called "Mute" Adams. Adams had ducked his head, Sunny Harper had lost no time in reining his horse around until he was close up to Mr. Sherrod's horse's tail, and the coyote, having watched with an interest no less than the cowboys' and having cocked his knowing eye at the bark chipped from a cedar some twenty or thirty feet above his head, moved on into the chaparral.

"I — I'm afraid I'm out of practice," sighed the marksman, returning his revolver to its holster and wiping his glasses with the tip end of his gay neck-scarf. "I'll have to put in a little time practising at a target."

It was that same evening, when the sun was just resting a broad golden disk upon the cliffs at the Lower

End and Mr. Sherrod was devoting himself patiently and painstakingly to the drilling of little holes in the atmosphere at a respectful distance from the ace of spades tacked to a young pine tree, that Bull Plummer rode up to the bunkhouse.

It was too early for the men to have come in from work. Only the owner, Sunny Harper and Cookie, busy at his stove, were in camp.

Sunny Harper, very joyous over the spectacle of the target-shooting and the cold which he was doctoring manfully with an ample dosage of whisky from the bottle which Mr. Sherrod had donated for its medicinal properties, saw Bull Plummer's big squat form rise above a knoll, stared, rubbed his eyes, regarded his bottle accusingly, and refused stubbornly to believe that he saw what he did see.

"If it was just Santy Claus coming," he murmured gently, "or a boy in brass buttons with a pitcher o' lemonade, or a couple elephants, I might believe it. But Bull Plummer — on this range? Shucks! This must be awful powerful licker!"

Sharply he cried out to Sherrod: "It's Bull Plummer! Now what in blue blazes do you reckon he's looking for?"

Sherrod did not seem to have seen or heard, so intent was he upon his revolver practice. Then a thing happened which made Sunny Harper choke upon his whisky; and to gag upon one's liquor was, in Mr. Harper's way of thinking, "a terrible unsportsmanlike proceeding." Sherrod, having missed his mark about three feet, squinted his eyes, set his teeth, and took long aim.

Harper, watching him, saw that Sherrod moved half a dozen quick steps to the right; surmised that still Sherrod was unaware of the approaching horsemen; noted furthermore that Sherrod's swift change of base brought the wavering muzzle of his big revolver to bear in the general direction of the man from the Bar Diamond.

"Hey there, Mr. Sherrod!" yelled the suddenly galvanized Sunny Harper, his mellowed soul in no mood to witness an accidental manslaughter, even though the victim be Plummer. "There comes Plummer! Look out, or — Oh, my God!"

He sat back weakly and shivered a little. Had Sherrod been blind or deaf? Had he not understood or had he not cared? The revolver in his hand spat flame, and its leaden missile, missing the tree more widely than its predecessors, sped on toward the man on horseback.

Yes; Sunny Harper gasped and choked and did not know that he did so. For he had seen an amazing thing. Sherrod's bullet had not missed Plummer's head three inches; it had torn a great, vicious hole in the peaked crown of Plummer's hat; it had carried the hat away and with it a lock of Plummer's black hair.

Plummer ducked wildly as a second bullet winged its way by his ear and announced his presence with a mighty shout, jerking his horse savagely back upon its haunches.

30

Sherrod, before he advanced toward the newcomer, turned for an instant to Harper.

"Plummer, you said it was, didn't you?" he asked softly.

"It sure is," grunted Sunny. "An' it makes me seasick thinking what chances I've took watching you shoot!"

Then Sherrod went to meet Plummer. Not, however, until Sunny Harper had seen his eyelid, the left eyelid, flutter downward behind his glasses in an unquestionable wink!

"Do you suppose," the astounded Sunny Harper communed within himself, "that he — he winked! Damn it, I seen it! He shot a hole in Plummer's hat and he says to me, 'Plummer, ain't he?' An' *he winked!*"

Slowly he lifted the bottle. Not to his lips, but up so that his wide eyes might stare at it. Slowly he put it down beside him, shaking his head.

"I don't give a hoot if I am drunk," he affirmed. "Sherrod popped a hole in Plummer's hat and then — he winked!"

Again Plummer was coming on swiftly. He had reined his horse about, leaned outward and downward from the saddle, had swept up his hat from the ground with an angry jerk, and now, his face red, his eyes roving restlessly about the bunkhouse, came up to Sherrod.

"What do you mean by this?" he snapped viciously.

"I say," laughed Sherrod, and the men who heard must guess as to whether the laugh was one of amusement or of nervousness, "I came pretty near getting you that shot, didn't I?"

"You sure did," growled Plummer, scowling briefly at his hat. "If you're lookin' for trouble —"

"Mercy!" cried Sherrod, shoving his gun back into its holster. "Don't you see? My target there — I was practising up. You came up unexpectedly. Looks like my shot went rather wild, doesn't it?"

"You're Sherrod, I take it?" grunted Plummer.

"Yes. You wanted to see me?"

He wiped his forehead, polished his glasses, and turned his eyes speculatively upon the Bar Diamond man. What they saw was a very heavy-set man upon a very beautiful horse.

The saddle-animal was black, young, spirited, groomed like a racehorse, legged like a greyhound. Sherrod's eyes swept the clean-cut lines of the horse admiringly and went curiously to Plummer. Here was a man larger than Hard Ross, thicker of neck, of arm, of thigh, of body. The bared throat was hairy, almost black with the tan of sun and air. The eyes were small and black, given unusual brilliance, beadlike, by the emotion which a moment ago had reddened his face; the mouth large, with heavy, slightly protruding under-lip.

Plummer's eyes, in the meantime, had found out Sunny Harper, where he sat cross-legged under a stunted oak, and had again come to rest upon Sherrod. Here they tarried, their gaze keen, intent, measuring.

"You see," said Sherrod pleasantly, "in shooting, as in anything else, practice makes perfect. I've come out here to stay, and a man living in this corner of the world ought to be a good shot, oughtn't he?"

32

Plummer nodded briefly. Again, before answering in words, he found time for a keen scrutiny which missed nothing of the conspicuous revolvers, the chaps which had remained so amazingly white, or the untouched ace of spades in the centre of a rudely scarred circle made by much flying lead, tacked to the tree. When he spoke it was a little contemptuously, as perhaps a cattleman could not have helped speaking, though he strove to make expression and voice alike pleasant.

"I'm Plummer, from the Bar Diamond," he explained. "Seein' as we're neighbours, I thought I'd drop over an' say 'Howdy.'"

"I'm glad you've come," cried Sherrod heartily. "Get down, Mr. Plummer. You've met Mr. Harper?"

"Oh, yes," returned Plummer easily, slipping out of the saddle and tossing his horse's reins to the ground. "Hello, Harper."

Sunny Harper's answer was a grunt which might have meant nothing or a very great deal. Plummer looked at him swiftly, shrugged his broad, sloping shoulders, and once more gave his attention to Sherrod.

"Like I said," repeated Plummer, looking straight and deep into Sherrod's unwavering eyes, "seeing as how we're neighbours, we ought to know each other."

"That's right," agreed Sherrod quickly. "I'm glad you came over."

"An' besides," went on Plummer in his slow, heavy drawl, "I wanted to talk business with you."

Sherrod's white fingers sought out a silver-chased cigarette case. "Business is dry work," he suggested mildly. "And you haven't had a drink yet. If Harper there doesn't need it all, we'll have a little drink to commemorate the occasion."

Plummer made no objection. Sunny Harper looked at his bottle with lingering affection, at the visitor with unconcealed dislike and distrust, and surrendered his cold-medicine with exceedingly bad grace.

A very few minutes later Bull Plummer again spoke of business. A couple of cigarettes had been smoked, the din of pans and pots from the cook's quarters told what that individual was about, the sun had slipped down behind the cliffs, and out in the valley some of the boys were riding toward rest and supper.

Sherrod seemed to hesitate a moment, and suggested:

"Suppose we go into my tent, Mr. Plummer? The boys are coming in and I think we could talk better out there."

A quick smile on Plummer's heavy lips told that he understood that his host realized he would not be a welcome guest when Hard Ross and the others arrived. He shrugged his shoulders again, and with no comment followed Sherrod to the little tent which the latter had helped with his own hands to pitch under a tree a hundred yards from the bunkhouse.

Sunny Harper, before the coming of the boys, had got to his feet and had walked to the well. He stumbled once and drew up frowning.

"I ain't drunk," he told himself severely. "I'm awful sober. If I keep my mouth shut, Ross ain't even going to smell my breath, he'll be that busy cogitating over Plummer's next move. But if I take him into my confidence, if I say to him, 'Ross, this new city boss of our'n just shot a hole in Plummer's hat — an' winked at me,' Ross is going to make a mistake an' say I'm drunk!"

Sunny went on, stumbled again, clapped his mouth tight shut and, when he drank from the well dipper, took his water between set teeth.

Just what passed that evening between the two men in the tent, the boys in the bunkhouse could not know. They knew that the owner of the Up and Down and the owner of the Bar Diamond talked long, and evidently with considerable earnestness. That alone was enough to drive Hard Ross into a fury of anger. In his way of thinking, Bull Plummer was several degrees lower in the scale than a coyote, a man who was crookeder than his reputation, and that was saying a very great deal.

"Sherrod ought to know it, too," he snarled over the meal which he did not know he was eating. "I've talked plain enough for a bonehead of a weak-eyed city guy to get wise. If he'd take a potshot at the low-down cattle thief with one of them young cannon of his, even if he missed him a mile an' shot his own foot off, I'd think the better of him."

Sherrod himself had come into the bunkhouse for something to eat for his guest and himself, had carried the plates and cups away, saying apologetically that they were very busy and could talk better out there alone.

And as they talked Bull Plummer's heavy voice grew always lower so that no chance word was blown upon

35

the evening breeze to the bunkhouse door, where the men went for their smokes. Steadily, as Plummer's tones sank, Sherrod's rose. Now and then a little gurgle of laughter came from him, and Sunny Harper thought begrudgingly of his cold-medicine.

"The four-eyed fool's getting drunk," he muttered disgustedly. "When you can measure a man by what little was left in that quart bottle, he ain't a man as you'd speak of with pride."

"Plummer ain't above stealing his stick-pin with the sparkler in it," growled Hard Ross. "An' I hope he does. Sh! What's that?"

No one answered as they all listened, for answer was superfluous. From the tent came the unmistakable click, click, click of poker chips being dropped into stacks by toying fingers.

Swiftly the darkness came on. There was a coal-oil lantern on the little table which Sherrod had placed by his bedside, and upon the tent walls were the silhouettes of the men whose business had gone the old way through the neck of a whisky bottle to a deck of cards. The table was between them now; Bull Plummer, sitting in the one chair, showed monstrously large against the white canvas; Sherrod, on the edge of the bed, again and again lifted a thick cup to his lips.

"Getting drunk an' playing Bull Plummer at the same time!" grunted Little John. "One guess to figger out what's going to happen."

"Same as a two-weeks'-old calf playing tag with a mountain wolf," offered a man whom they called

"Needles," one not usually guilty of idle remarks, a man given to silence like his side-kick, "Mute" Adams.

The click of the poker chips continued. Before long the musical chink of gold and silver added its account of what was happening. It grew late, and the game went on. Happy Day Tennant yawned, stretched his short arms as far as was physically possible above his round body, and went to bed. One by one the others followed him.

Still the game went on, and Hard Ross alone sat on the doorstep, a cigarette dead between his lips, his eyes frowning and bent steadily upon the shadow shapes.

The stars floated out into a dark heaven absolutely cloudless, the little wind died down, the moon at the full paused a moment over the steep cliffs standing like Titan-piled walls at the Upper End, then moved its golden way through the golden stars, and still the game went on and Hard Ross watched and waited. He didn't see the stars, and he hadn't noticed the moon. His thoughts were full of Bull Plummer and Sherrod, of Hawley and a mare named Silver Slippers.

"Bull Plummer knows just where Silver Slippers is right now," muttered Hard Ross heavily. "He knows where more'n one long-horn wearing a U and D brand on its hide has gone the last year. He knows I know it. An' he's got the nerve to show up here, right under my nose! He'd ought to know it ain't real safe to monkey aroun' on the Up an' Down while I'm on the job an' while the rest of the boys is feeling strong enough to walk. Now, what's his play? What did he come for? Huh?"

The play was made; what did it mean? Bull Plummer had come to the range, and he had said that it was just to get acquainted with his new neighbour. That made Hard Ross want to laugh. Plummer wasn't in the habit of riding ten miles of hard trail just to pay a social call.

Ross made one cigarette after another and sat still, staring at the colossal shadow of the man he distrusted. The hours slipped by, the click of chips and jingle of coins continued. It was on the edge of midnight when the big shadow straightened up, and Sherrod threw back the flap of the tent.

Ross, in the shadows of the bunkhouse, did not move. He pinched out the fire of his cigarette and watched the two men as they moved away toward the horse which Plummer had left to wait for him during the hours of his stay without grain or water. He saw that Plummer walked swiftly, steadily, turning his head this way and that like a man suspicious of danger. He saw that Sherrod lurched a little, that once he laid his hand on his companion's arm, and guessed what he had guessed before, that Sherrod had drunk most of the whisky.

He heard a brief conversation end as Plummer swung up into the saddle, heard Sherrod agree to ride over to the Bar Diamond for another game, and with tight-set lips watched the big man ride away through the shadows of the moonlight night.

Sherrod, still swaying a little, turned from Plummer and walked unsteadily toward the tent. Hard Ross, springing to his feet, went with long strides to the new owner's side.

"He skinned you nice an' plenty, I reckon," snorted the foreman. "Huh?"

Sherrod's amiable smile showed weak in the wan light.

"Come on inside the tent, Ross, that's a good fellow," came the answer as unsteady as the man's walk. "Want to tell you about it."

Ross followed as Sherrod led a devious way. Within the tent Sherrod threw himself upon the bed murmuring.

"He's a fine fellow, Plummer. Great fellow."

"That's all right," cut in Ross sharply. "You can't tell me much about him I don't know already." His stern eyes ran quickly from table littered with cards and chips to overturned chair and empty bottle. "Tell me what happened."

"Great chappie, Plummer," Sherrod wandered on absently. "Plays fine hand of cards. And I know, Ross. I'm no baby myself when it comes to the good old game, you know. I'm going over to his home; we're going to play some more. Better come along, Ross, old chap."

"Tell me what happened!" snapped Ross, losing patience. "How much did he skin you out of?"

"Oh!" Sherrod laughed unevenly. "How much did he skin me out of? Why, let me see."

He sat up, adjusted the nose-glasses which had slipped awry, and ran his fingers into his vest pockets. Then he stood on his feet and put his hands into his trousers pockets, swaying dangerously. The smile gradually broadened on his face.

"Say, Ross, don't tell the boys," he chuckled. "He played the greatest run of luck you ever saw. He's the luckiest man dealing cards I ever saw. On my deals it wasn't so bad. Yes, sir." His laugh made Ross's hands clench. "Every time he'd deal me a hand, I thought my luck had changed, the hand was so good. And then his would be better, and he'd win! Talk about a man's lucky night!"

"How much did he win?" thundered Ross.

"Why," hazarded Sherrod, smiling. "About five hundred, I'd say. He —"

But Hard Ross had swept back the tent flap and was running toward the stable.

"What's the matter?" called Sherrod after him. "Where are you going, Ross? What's the hurry? Let me tell you —"

"I'm goin' to get my horse an' go for a little ride," Ross's angry voice boomed back at him. "An' you better go to bed an' put your clothes under your pillow, so some jasper don't come an' skin you out'n them."

Hard Ross wasn't always in a towering rage. There were times when he sang — at least Ross accounted it singing. There were times when, in affable humour, he made jokes and perhaps the worst puns that were ever made. But here of late it seemed to him that most happenings conspired to put him into the mood to chew tenpenny nails. As if he didn't have trouble enough on his hands without the advent of this four-eyed fool, Sherrod!

The Up and Down ranch was Hard Ross's life. The, late owner, Hodges, would let two or three years pass

40

without showing up; Ross, quite excusably, got into the way of figuring that the spread was his. He took his job seriously. He didn't mean that anyone, Bull Plummer or another, should put anything over on the Up and Down. Then look at to-night! Just look at it! Bull Plummer had made a howling jackass out of the new owner; that meant that he had thumbed his nose at the Up and Down. And again Hard Ross was good and mad.

"He can't do that to me," said Ross, and rode.

It was a night of big fat clouds and a moon, so at times he rode in the dark and at other times in bright spots of moonlight. He realized that Bull Plummer had a good head-start; but then, Hard Ross was in the greater hurry since he knew what was ahead of him and Plummer did not in the least suspect what was following him.

"No, sir, he can't do that to me," said Ross again. It didn't strike him that it had been done to Sherrod, perhaps even to the Up and Down. Dammit, who ran the Up and Down and was responsible for everything on it? Hard Ross, nobody else.

Once in a while poor old Hard Ross groaned; he couldn't help it. Why did he have to have a boss like this Sherrod, a man whom, it seemed, he'd have to nurse like a baby? Why did the doggone fool have to give his shirt to Bull Plummer, the man who was already robbing him?

"Maybe I'm getting soft," grumbled Ross. "Maybe I ought to go back right now and cut Sherrod's throat for him, and get it over the easiest way, the shortest and best way."

But it stuck in his craw that Plummer had ridden off with five hundred dollars, Up and Down money, and that Plummer, getting Sherrod cock-eyed, had cheated him out of every cent. No, Plummer couldn't do that to him — meaning Hard Ross. The devil take Sherrod, anyway. But there was the Up and Down ranch to be remembered, and there was its foreman, and Bull Plummer wasn't going to laugh at either of them. Not long, anyhow.

So Hard Ross dipped his spurs and made the best time he could, always watching the patches of moonlight for a sight of the man who rode on ahead.

Ross caught sight of Plummer just in time to see him meet somebody riding down the valley. He saw Plummer rein in across the trail and stop. The other rider, so narrow was the trail there, stopped perforce.

Ross heard their voices through the stillness. He sat his horse at the edge of a grove of gay, shimmering young aspens that were tipped at the top with moonshine and cloaked in darkness below. Ross stopped discreetly in the shadows and listened.

He heard Plummer say — and he even saw how Plummer, in his clumsy way, pulled his hat off.

"Oh, hello, Miss Dawn! It's you, is it? Where do you think you are going this time of night?"

The girl's voice, though she spoke softly, came to Hard Ross clearly.

"Mr. Plummer, isn't it? It was just such a lovely night that I had to go for a ride. You're going home, aren't you? Well, I'll ride a little farther down the valley and then go home, too. Good night, Mr. Plummer."

"Oh, look here, Dawn," said Plummer. "There's no rush; you're in no hurry and neither am I. Let's ride along together. Anywhere you say."

The girl answered — and Ross thought that her throat had tightened — he thought that she was frightened and did not want Plummer to know. She said, fairly steadily:

"Thank you, Mr. Plummer. But I know you are homeward bound. And then, too, don't you know how it is when one wants to be all alone? Just to ride and sort of drift along and not to have to do any thinking. Good night."

Plummer shot his hand out and gripped her wrist. Hard Ross saw that, too.

"Dawn!"

The girl wrenched away. Hard Ross saw her lift her quirt. And that was all he needed to see.

Much to Bull Plummer's surprise, about two minutes later he had not only a girl on a lonesome trail to deal with, but the foreman of the Up and Down.

"Miss Dawn," said Hard Ross, "you ride on anywhere you please. Me and Plummer has got some business to talk over, awful confidential business, Miss Dawn. So you just ride. And if I was you, I'd streak straight back home — and I wouldn't go riding all alone this time of night."

"Mr. Ross! You're Mr. Hard Ross, aren't you?"

"That's me," said Ross. "And now will you head home?"

"But —"

"There ain't no buts," said Ross, and grew impatient. "You ought to know when you're well out of a jam — so use your spurs."

Still she hesitated: She saw trouble brewing; Ross's voice gave her the first clue, Bull Plummer's absolute silence proved the case.

"I'll go if you'll ride with me, Mr. Ross," she decided to say.

"Can't," said Ross. "Me and Plummer will be talking here long enough for you to be as good as home. Ride, won't you?"

"But, Mr. Ross —"

"I told you there wasn't any buts. Make up your mind. Am I going to turn tail and leave you and Plummer together? Or are you going to get going?"

She said quite simply, "Thank you, Hard Ross. I'm glad that you came. And I know that everything is going to be all right with you."

"It always is!" Ross called after her as she reined about and shot back along the up-trail.

Hard Ross was in no mood, feeling impatient and disgruntled, to take any unnecessary chances. So he had a gun in his hand; in a shaft of moonlight Bull Plummer saw its ugly nose resting on the horn of Hard Ross's saddle.

"Bull Plummer," said Hard Ross, "I'm here to tell you something. Matter of fact, I rode all this way to have a nice little talk with you. And while I'm talking,

44

you better not waggle an eyebrow, or I'll shoot you through the gizzard."

"What the hell's eating you, Ross? Gone crazy?"

"I don't like the way you wear your face, Bull Plummer. I don't like the way you talk to a nice girl. I don't like the way you play poker. I sort of guess I don't like anything about you."

"You're drunk, you fool!"

"No. For one thing, I don't like you slapping down your feet on Up and Down land."

Bull Plummer laughed at him.

"You! You've had your free hand with that ranch quite a spell now, haven't you, Ross? But old man Hodges is out, and Sherrod is in — and I happened to be Sherrod's guest! Visiting your boss, Mr. Hard Ross. Get that in your nut, will you? Now quit sticking your damned gun in my general direction and be on your way, cowboy."

"I've been responsible for that outfit, like you say, a good many years, Bull Plummer. Now this Johnny-come-lately, name of Sherrod, buys the place. Just the same he keeps me on as foreman. So it's still up to me. And if you think you can come back, long as I'm holding down my job, just think again; orders to the boys is to shoot all coyotes on sight, including Bull Plummer. Another thing —"

"Oh, shut up," said Plummer. "Dry up and blow away cowboy. I've got places to go, and —"

"And there's this," said Hard Ross. "I don't like you to come and get the boss drunk and steal his money. It's five hundred bones you lifted off the damn fool to-night. Well, fork it over; I'll take it back to him. Get busy, Plummer."

Plummer's laugh, full of contempt and mockery, preluded Plummer's answer.

"Any time, Ross!" he jibed. "You'd take it back to him, would you? Or maybe stick it in your own jeans? What do you take me for, anyhow?"

"For a low-life, a polecat, and the sort that would hold up a decent girl on a lonely trail. Now, fork over, Plummer. The wind's blowing from you to me, and I don't like the smell of it; I want to be on my way."

Plummer shifted in the saddle. Ross's gun, lifted now a few inches above his saddle horn, did not shift.

Plummer, enraged, said hoarsely, "I'll see you in hell first, you —"

"No you won't," Ross told him evenly. "I've got the drop on you, and you know it. And just a half-excuse for filling you full of lead is all I need. Dig, Plummer!"

"Am I going to dig my own grave?" roared Plummer. "The money is in my tail pocket. The minute I dropped my hand down to my pants, you'd take your chance and pop a bullet through me! I'm no sucker like that, Hard Ross!"

Hard Ross sat very still a moment. Then, in what moonlight there was, a golden shaft across his face, Plummer saw his broadening grin. Ross said gravely:

"So the money's in your pants pocket, huh? Well, I reckon it would be. So suppose, Mr. Plummer, that you slide down out of the saddle, take your pants off, and hand them to me with whatever's in them! It's an idea! Then you can ride along home!"

46

Plummer, his rage burning hotter than ever, made a quick gesture toward his hip. Hard Ross promptly shot a hole in the air within an inch or two of Bull Plummer's right ear.

"Kind of bad shooting," said Ross. "But then, the light ain't so good, sort of tricky you know. Next time I can do better." Then his voice hardened. "Pile out of your saddle damn quick and do what I say, or, so help me, I'll kill you!" he said.

There was no temporising when a voice like that issued such simple orders. Plummer slipped down from the saddle, unbuckled his belt, kicked off his nether garments, and flung them at Hard Ross. Ross caught them neatly over his arm. His hand explored the pockets; it found what he wanted. He said, "Get on your horse and ride, Plummer. And when you get home, just tell the boys you got so scared you jumped clean out of your pants! Ride, Plummer, before I start shooting your bootheels off. And remember, you don't come back any more to the Up and Down."

Plummer mounted and rose. An undignified sight, judged Hard Ross who sent an unkind but heartfelt gale of laughter after him.

CHAPTER
FIVE

Sherrod awoke with a start. It was very dark, and his frowning eyes could scarcely make out the blurred form he could hear moving within his tent. Then there was a spurt of a match, and before the lantern was lighted he knew that here was Hard Ross returned from his ride.

He lay still, saying nothing, his eyes striving for a view of the foreman's face. When at last the features stood out from the thick darkness, Sherrod saw that Hard Ross's lips were tightly compressed, that his eyes were stern and wrathful.

"I must say," began the man on the bed, sitting up against his pillows, "you've got strange nocturnal habits, my dear fellow! To go for a ride at midnight, for one thing; to come in here and wake me up, for another."

"An' it strikes me I ain't the only man on this range," retorted Ross sharply, "who's got the habit of doing almighty funny things."

He ran a big hand across his forehead and came closer to Sherrod's bed, towering over him.

"Here's your money," he said bluntly. He drew from his pocket a handful of gold and silver and dropped it upon the little table. "You might count it to see if I lost any."

"What!" cried Sherrod incredulously. He was sitting up very straight now, and his eyes had widened perceptibly. "You mean that that is why you rode after Plummer? You held him up!"

"I stuck him up just as pretty as if I'd been highwayman for ten years," grunted Hard Ross. "An' now I'm going to bed. But first I'm going to tell you something, Mr. Sherrod."

"Go ahead," returned Sherrod, watching him wonderingly and making no move to count the confusion of coins. "To say that I'm curious would be drawing it rather mild, Ross."

"It's just this: I ain't ever saw a growed-up man that was a greener tenderfoot than you in all my born days, an' I don't expect to live long enough to see you beat. But that ain't worrying me. That's your funeral. If you want to let a crook come an' skin you out'n your pile on a string of raw deals —"

"You don't mean to insinuate," cut in Sherrod, "that Plummer wasn't playing fair? That he cheated?"

"No, I ain't. And that's because I ain't got a word like insinuate in my head where my tongue can reach for it. I'm just saying he's as high up in the order of thieving crooks as you are in the club of damn fool tenderfeet. All the same, not caring whether you buy aigs with your money an' let a yeller dog suck the aigs, I goes out an' makes Mr. Bull Plummer look into the open end of a little forty-four, an' brings back your customers to you. An' I don't want to be misunderstood none. I want you to know why I done a play like that!"

"I'm certainly very anxious to know," remarked Sherrod stiffly.

He sought for his nose-glasses, found them, stuck them upon his nose, and directed a keen glance through them upon his foreman.

"An' I'm telling you, ain't I? We been losing considerable stock from the Up an' Down, off an' on for quite a spell. That stock ain't been climbing over the cliffs looking for eagles' nests, an' they ain't been diving into the lakes looking for trout. They've been stole, stole from right under my nose. On top of that, a couple of weeks ago Silver Slippers, the finest little mare you ever seen, gets stole out'n the barn right down here. Now, I ain't a mind reader, maybe, but I ain't exactly what you'd call a blind man, neither. I know who the crook is, back of the whole deal. An' do I look like a man as is going to let that same crook come riding right square into camp an' stick the owner of the Up and Down for five hundred bucks an' then get away with it, laughing at *me* all the time?" Ross's big fists were doubled, his eyes threatening. "He didn't laugh none when I overtook him on the trail an' had my little talk with him!"

"But, man alive!" cried Sherrod. "You don't mean that you suspect Plummer of being a cattle thief? Why, he's a rancher like me; he told me to-night that he's been losing stock, too. He even suggested that we get together and formulate some scheme of apprehending

50

the rustlers. Why, Ross, that is the business he came over on!"

"An' you swallowed that?" demanded Ross in mingled wonder and contempt.

"Let me tell you something, my friend," said Sherrod impatiently. "As soon as it is morning I'm going to ride over to the Bar Diamond. I am going to take this money back to Mr. Plummer, and I'm going to apologise to him for your conduct of to-night. And then —"

"It don't make no manner of difference to me what you do," cut in Ross angrily. "An' it don't make no difference to me what Plummer does, just so he keeps off this range as long as I'm foreman here, an' just so he don't take nothing off'n the range as don't belong to him."

"But, look here, Ross —"

"I'm going to bed," Ross snapped back at him. And Ross went to bed.

When he had gone Mr. Sherrod lay very still for a long time, his eyes full of speculation as they rested upon the money on the table. Then he took off his glasses, put them by the money, put out his light, and lay back, laughing softly.

"I'd like to know just what was said on the trail," he chuckled.

And then he went to sleep.

In the morning the expected happened when Sherrod complained of a headache and besought Cookie, at a late hour, to bring him a cup of coffee, very black.

Cookie grinned and brought the coffee. His eyes flew wide open at the sight of the money scattered upon the table.

Sherrod groaned, found his nose-glasses, which with trembling fingers he stuck upon his nose, saw the money through them, and in return for Cookie's kindness invited him to help himself to a dollar or so. Cookie made it four dollars and went his way back to the bunkhouse whistling and meditating upon a little trip to White Rock.

The boys had gone about the day's work. Half an hour after the coffee had been drunk, Sherrod came into the bunkhouse. He made a rather good meal then, and smoked a cigarette. And then he prepared for his ride, for the returning of a call and five hundred dollars poker money.

He shaved and spent much time removing a spot from his white chaps. He brought to light a new silk shirt, this one a bright red, and selected a very beautiful white silk neckerchief to go with it. Then, his money in his pocket, his two revolvers bumping grandly against his hips, his spurs twinkling in the morning sunlight, he went down to the corral, cornered his horse, caught him with coaxing words and a wisp of hay, saddled and rode away toward the Upper End.

It was a wonderful morning, and Sherrod, as he rode his gentle horse through the valley, sang little snatches of song and looked about him with brightening glances. He had before him some five miles before he came to the Upper End, where the steep cliffs closed in about the Twin Lakes, another five miles or so to ride through the pass, over the south ridge and to the Bar Diamond headquarters. His trail followed the willow-fringed creek which, after slipping through its rock-bound gorges where it had its source in the Twin Lakes, ran its merry race westward to water the meadows of the Up and Down.

Upon leaving the Up and Down bunkhouse behind him, Sherrod rode into what the boys called Big Tree Meadow. Here the valley widened abruptly, here the floor was level and studded with venerable cedars and sugar pines, their outflung branches tossed so high against the sky that a man under them lost sight of the rock walls of the valley two or three miles away from him on right and left. Half an hour's leisurely progress through Big Tree Meadow brought horse and rider to the Narrows, where again the cliffs drew closer in on each hand until little more than a mile separated them.

Through the Narrows Sherrod rode on, touching his ambling horse with the spur and breaking into a gallop. He noticed how the cliffs, rising almost perpendicularly along the boundary lines of the range, were impossible of crossing for cattle and horses.

"Lots of fence was saved when this valley was made," he meditated.

The mountain barriers extended on either hand almost in parallel lines until he had ridden into the Gap. Here the cliffs were not five hundred yards apart on each side, and through them, rushing downward from a rocky shelf, the creek made its leaping descent in the white froth of waterfalls. Here the trail became suddenly steep and difficult, winding back and forth along the rising precipices, at times so narrow that the rider's leg scraped against the rocks, and a twig let fall from his right hand dropped straight a hundred feet into the whirlpools.

Again he came of a sudden upon a level, tree-studded plateau, and then all unheralded, upon the bright beauty of Twin Lakes. One of them half a mile long, the other a very little less, the overflow of the first created the second, just as the surplus waters of the second made the creek. Fringed with monster pines and cedars mirrored in their placid surfaces, the homes of big trout, the watering places of the wild animals from the uplands, the two lakes lay before their new owner like great, glorious jewels in a setting of emerald. For everywhere, hanging down from the cliffs which towered straight into air half a thousand feet about the still water, masking the rugged harshness of the towering boulders and carpeting the ground at the foot of pine and cedar, was a screen of vines, a mat of moss. And in the little recesses which time and weather had carved into the rock walls and whence many a clear, cool spring trickled, ferns stood thick and tall, and lush-stemmed flowers lifted their yellow and their red heads.

It was a fairy nook, and this morning under the warm blue sky should have been peopled with fairies. Sherrod reined in his horse and sat very still in the saddle looking upon this corner of his possessions admiringly.

"It's worth all that the range cost me," he said under his breath. Which went to indicate that perhaps Sherrod was not altogether a fool and a blind man.

He rode on upon a narrow, grass-grown trail and once more drew rein to look down upon the lake whose shores he had skirted, and also upon the other lakelet lying just before him. He listened to the murmur of waters as it blended with the droning murmur of treetops, and found music in it.

For close to a quarter of an hour he sat very still. His eyes, keen and frowning, travelled back and forth along the base of the cliffs, seeming to be seeking something. This was the first time he had come to this end of his holdings, and perhaps he sought the trail which led from here through a pass and into the Bar Diamond country.

But his eyes were still frowning, still seeking, when at last he touched his horse with the spur and rode on. His trail led him to the Upper Lake. He paused again, looking at the tiny island which seemed to be afloat upon the middle of the water's quiet surface, an island which was but the upthrust crest of a submerged knoll, tree crowned and not measuring fifty paces from edge to edge.

From the miniature isle it was the logical thing for his eyes to wander across the upper lake to the far side and to the beetling cliffs. And so he found something which mildly surprised him since he had not expected to find it here.

It was a cabin built of squared logs and set close to the base of granite cliff behind it so that the cliff really constituted the rear wall of the little dugout. For scarcely more than dugout was it, a poor enough shack covering a square of ground ten feet across from side to side.

"A camp for the boys when they have to spend a night up at this end," guessed Sherrod.

At first he saw no way to get to the cabin across the lake. It stood upon a rocky ledge, a bare space of some twenty yards intervening between it and the edge of the water. But presently he noted that his trail led from where he was around the farther shore and to the cabin door. And he saw, too, not a hundred yards from the cabin where the pass which he sought led through a narrow cañon and on toward the Bar Diamond outfit.

And he saw something else. And that something else so surprised the newcomer to this corner of the West that he gasped his astonishment. It was the strangest building, if "building" it could be called, that he had ever seen.

It was between the mouth of the pass and the lone cabin. It was but little over a couple of hundred of yards from him when first he saw it, but it was really understandable why he had not seen it before, and this despite its very considerable size.

Had the thing stood in the heart of a city it would have loomed up more conspicuously, more marked and more distinctive than a record-breaking skyscraper. It would have caught the eye a mile away. But here, in the heart of the wild, Sherrod had almost stumbled upon it without seeing it. That was because it was built so that it seemed a part of the wilderness, at one with it, making no discord in the harmony of the landscape. Its pillars were the shaggy boles of giant trees, with the rough bark and green moss still upon them. Its walls were of the same native logs, or of the grey granite boulders bestrewing the slopes. One corner column was a living cedar whose green boughs high above stirred gently in a breeze which did not sift down to the surface of the lake. One corner was a shoulder of the granite cliff.

The odd structure did not look to be the work of man; it seemed rather some dryad-home grown into being as the trees and the rocks themselves had grown. And in reality it was the abode of man, man-made, large enough to shelter at one time all of the men who had ever come into the valley of the Twin Lakes.

"The man who dreamed that thing into being," muttered the surprised Sherrod, "was an artist. And I have never heard of it! There should be woodland nymphs in a place like this; that is where their Lady Queen should have her throne room."

To register a mental picture of the whole required but an instant when once it had stood apart in his vision from the forest and cliffs; to appreciate each little detail, to grasp the significance of each one, kept him motionless in the saddle, staring.

He saw where a window looked out through the branches of a gnarled cedar, vine-framed; saw where what appeared to be but a spire of rock was in fact a deep-throated chimney giving exit to a thin wisp of blue smoke; saw that what he first mistook for a chance-fallen log, lightning-blasted, was a rustic footbridge spanning one of the many bickering streams which slipped down into the lake; and wondered as he made out that the stream, stealing forth into the sunlight from between two big boulders, came from within the sylvan house.

The clear, laughing waters flashing into the sunlight from some unseen source within the strange dwelling spoke to his fancy of a nature-made fountain in some spacious courtyard grass carpeted, fern-rimmed, starred with wild flowers.

Now, more than ever, was there need for the queen of these solitudes.

And there was within him a sense of deep satisfaction, of the utter, complete fitness of things, rather than any great surprise, when his questing eyes found her.

CHAPTER
SIX

She had seen Sherrod before he had more than realized that she should be here to make the scene perfect. Without her, this nook of the mountains was like some rare setting without its jewel; with her, the vision was complete, exquisitely perfected.

Beside the stream upon which his admiring eyes had rested there was a huge granite block, rudely squared, flat-topped. Two fir trees grew close together upon one side of it, dropping their black shadows upon the level surface. And in their shade, not fifty yards from him, some ten feet above the surface of the stream, gracefully idle as she lay upon a great brown bearskin, watching him with amused eyes, was the maiden.

"Good morning," said Sherrod quietly, lifting his hat with something of a flourish as he spurred his horse nearer to the granite block. "Good morning — provided that be the proper salutation."

"If you are in doubt as to the time of the day, it isn't anywhere near noon yet," she assured him gravely.

He saw that she was dressed very becomingly in something dove-coloured, although his man's eyes did not concern themselves with feminine details in the matter of the tying of a hair ribbon or the mode of a pattern. His man's eyes did concern themselves very particularly, however, with the white of her rounded throat, the brown of her hair through which the sun had scattered much shimmering gold, the bronzed, clear-skinned cheeks, the very red lips, stained with youth and curved to laughter, and with her eyes. He was near enough now to marvel at the soft grey of their colouring, to fancy that he could see the little golden flecks in them like tiny glints of sunlight.

"My doubt was merely concerning the form of address to be used when one meets the Queen of the Dryads," he returned soberly. "A 'good morning,' seems somehow not exactly to fit the occasion, you know. I was undecided whether I should go poetic with something like, 'Forgive the impudence of mine eyes, O Spirit of the Woodland!' or whether I should seek flowers to strew before you, calling devoutly, 'All hail, Dawn Maiden!'"

"So then you know who I am?" was what she said, puzzling him. And as she read further perplexity in the eyes turned gravely upon her through the nose-glasses which he had put on at first sight of her, she added lightly, "Suppose we just say good morning, Mr. Sherrod? You are Mr. Sherrod, aren't you?"

"I know only what you seem to be, not who you are," he returned, a little surprised that she called him Mr. Sherrod. "As for you, I suppose your trees and streams and mountain breezes tell you the names of presumptuous mortals daring to invade your fast-nesses?"

60

He swung down from his saddle, left his horse with dragging reins, and stepped across the log bridge so that he stood on the rude rock steps leading up to her. He saw now that her feet were incased in little deerskin moccasins decorated with Indian beadwork, and that a book had slipped from her hand and lay unheeded upon the bear rug.

"I hope that you will forgive my invasion of your solitude," he said when he stood halfway up the uneven ascent and his eyes were level with hers. "Yes, I am Sherrod of the Up and Down."

He paused a moment as if inviting a like confidence, and when all that he got was a sweeping glance, full of quiet laughter, which ran from his silken scarf nicely tied, to the broad belt and the butt of a revolver just showing when she sat upright, he flushed a little and went on hurriedly:

"I'm the new owner of the range, as perhaps you have heard? I've been here only a couple of weeks and until this morning never rode so far this way."

She nodded and made no answer. The laughter had gone from her eyes, and she was looking out across the lake now, musingly. Sherrod was not quite comfortable, not quite certain that she had not forgotten that he was on her side of the cliffs. He bit his lip, hesitated a little, and then went on stubbornly:

"I had the idea that my land comprised all of the territory within this basin, that it extended quite across the lake and beyond the cliffs. You see, I bought the range on what I knew of it and without actually riding over it. I had never heard of the unique building which is, I take it, your home?"

He wasn't sure that she so much as nodded this time. He saw the curve of her cheek, and it told him nothing. And still he continued:

"Evidently I was mistaken. Am I asking too much if I request that you tell me just where my boundary line is? Am I tresspassing on another man's property right now?"

Her head turned slowly, he saw her profile, then her eyes were turned searchingly upon him. For the moment that she did not reply he felt that she was trying to look down under the surface of him, trying to make out what manner of man he really was.

"No doubt it is a little confusing," she admitted quietly. "Yes, the Up and Down range does include the lake, Mr. Sherrod. Both lakes. And your line does run to the top of the cliffs, I think, something like half or three-quarters of a mile beyond. Still," she added with a faint hint of a smile which came and was gone so swiftly that Sherrod was not sure that his eyes had not tricked him into thinking a beam of quivering sunlight down through the branches was a smile, "I am very much afraid that you are trespassing. Just adjoining your range on the east there is a quarter-section which belongs to us. Our hundred and sixty acres are mostly those cliffs yonder," nodding to the rocky fall of mountains back of them, at the extreme eastern end of the valley. "About two acres of our little place, however, are down here. We extend almost to your Upper Lake."

62

She went on in the same quiet matter-of-fact tone to indicate certain natural landmarks standing between the border of the Up and Down and what she was pleased to term the "place belonging to us." So Sherrod noted that one end of the log bridge lay upon his property, the other end upon "ours," and understood that when he had passed over the middle of the stream he had begun to trespass.

He saw that the strange rambling dwelling which seemed so intimate a part of the wilderness was just beyond his line. Then he glanced across the lake, understanding that the tiny tree-topped island was all his; his eyes came to rest upon the sturdy cabin of squared logs which he had first seen.

"That is mine or yours?" he asked.

He knew that he didn't care whose it was; he fully realized that he wouldn't have given fifteen cents for it; but he had no mind yet to end his conversation with her.

"Yours, I suppose." She seemed to hesitate, and then as she went on a little flush crept into her cheeks. "Father had it built, I believe. Oh, long years ago before our real home had grown. People didn't think much of boundary lines in those days. And, even now, he uses it for a sort of storeroom. I hope you won't mind?"

"I say," cut in Sherrod hastily. "I don't care anything about boundary lines, myself. That's all right. I just asked —"

"To keep the conversation going?" she suggested with another of her quick, elusive smiles.

"Well," he retorted bluntly, "why not? I did want to talk with you, to be neighbourly — for we are neighbours, aren't we? And you didn't seem in the least eager to do your part."

"If my part is to talk with a young gentleman I've never seen before and consequently could not, by the largest stretch of all that's reasonable, have the slightest interest in, no," she answered him as bluntly.

"But I've never seen you before, either, have I? And I'm interested in you."

She shrugged a very lovely pair of shoulders and her hand went to the book she had dropped before he came and had forgotten afterward.

"The proper thing to say, I suppose," she said lightly. "And now, Mr. Sherrod, if there are no more questions you wish to put to me —"

"But there are," he returned imperturbably. "Two questions more, if you will be so kind as to answer them for me. The first is, can you tell me if that is the trail yonder" — he pointed to the pass which he had noted leading southward — "which leads to the Bar Diamond?"

He saw a quick flash of interest in the big grey eyes when he mentioned the Bar Diamond, and he was wondering what should bring that light into them when it was as suddenly veiled by the sweep of her lashes.

"That is the trail," she answered, making no comment.

"And the other question," he continued quietly, "is may I call sometime?"

64

"That," she said with pointed indifference, "is a matter which you had best take up with Father, hadn't you? If you wish to be neighbourly with him, no doubt —"

"I should like to call on you," he told her equably.

"You are very kind, Mr. Sherrod. And I should be delighted if — if calls weren't such a nuisance. Honestly, don't you think that they are? In town we put up with such things, just as we eat and drink things which we don't like, merely to please a hostess who doesn't care a snap about it, and wear gowns and hats because they are fashionable, when they look hideous and feel uncomfortable. Maybe you haven't lived out here in the wilderness long enough to realize that it isn't necessary to be polite. So, you see there is no real reason why you should ask to call or why I should say I should be delighted."

She stood up, her finger lost in the leaves of her book, and looked down upon his upturned face, her eyes mystifying him.

"Conventionalities are really very little, insignificant things in the shadow of cliffs like those big old fellows," she ended the matter.

Or sought to end it. For there appeared to be a strain of stubbornness in Sherrod's make-up. He watched the graceful, slow movements of her supple young body as she came toward him, saw the moccasined foot seek the topmost of the rude steps and put out his own slender, white hand to her. She did not seem to notice it, her gown brushed against his chaps, and she passed down, neither hurriedly not loiteringly.

"I must be going in," she said when she had passed him. "Good-bye, Mr. Sherrod."

"You might at least tell me your name," he said a trifle irritably. "And you might let me know when I can call."

"Wouldn't it simplify matters if you didn't call? Then you wouldn't have any need of knowing my name."

"But I want to see you again."

"Very much, I suppose?" and there was a hint of laughter in her voice.

"Very, very much," he returned.

He, too, had come down the steps and stood looking after her, his eyes filled with an admiration which there was no need to hide since she had not turned toward him. But now she paused a moment and did turn, so swiftly that the admiration was still high in his eyes.

"If you want to see me very much," she said in mock seriousness, "you may come."

"It is very kind of you to let me call —"

"I didn't say *call.* I said once before that calls are stupid, and all people who are not stupid themselves know it."

She bestowed upon him a long, sweeping, leisurely glance which might have been a trifle impertinent, and which took stock of his broad hat, his theatrical cowboy costume, ending with a little twitch of the lips when her eyes rested upon the dainty black boots, the remarkably high heels, the amazingly ornate silver spurs.

"If you want to see me very much, you can prove it."

Sherrod adjusted his nose-glasses with precision and returned her cool glance coolly.

66

"But give me the opportunity, Dawn Maiden," he said soberly.

A quick frown came into her eyes.

"Why do you call me that?" she demanded a bit stiffly.

Sherrod laughed.

"For two reasons; I always have two reasons for everything, you know. First, you will remember that, although I asked for your name, you refused it. Second, you look like that."

"And you really don't know what my name is?"

"No. But you were going to tell me how I could prove to you that I want very much to see you again?"

"Yes. I have been thinking all day that I'd like to see the sun come up in the morning from Daybreak Spire. I shall be there just before the sun rises; I shall leave right after sunrise and hurry back for breakfast. You may come to see me there. And if you do," and the laughter was all unsuppressed now, "I'll bring you back to have breakfast with me, Mr. Sherrod!"

"But where is Daybreak Spire?" he called to her. For she had turned again and was moving away from him.

"I am not answering any more questions to-day, kind sir," she retorted. "Good-bye, Mr. Sherrod."

"Then, I'll find out," Sherrod told her. And when she did not seem to have heard, he called louder, "If I needed proof, your to-morrow morning's jaunt to watch the sun come up proves that you *are* the Dawn Maiden!"

He watched her move upward along the stream's course, saw her pass upon its brink between the two big boulders which formed a strange portal to the strange house.

Then she disappeared without once turning. And Sherrod swung up to his horse's back and rode on through the shadows of the great trees to the mouth of the pass leading over the cliffs and to the Bar Diamond.

And from between the boles of two giant cedars standing at the side of the big boulders a pair of very merry grey eyes watched him until the spotlessly white chaps and brilliantly red silk shirt and twinkling spurs had passed out of sight.

"I wonder what he is up to?" murmured the Dawn Maiden, her book lying forgotten where she had tossed it upon a pile of cushions. "You may be a very great fool, Mr. Sherrod; I rather think you are a very clever young man. Anyway, your nose-glasses . . . Most of the time you look under them or over them — and not through them!"

Then a voice, a man's voice, called sharply to her. And answering, "Yes," a frown coming again into her eyes, she went to answer more questions and tell of her encounter with the new owner of the Up and Down.

CHAPTER
SEVEN

Sherrod found his ride through the pass, over the ridge, and down into the Bar Diamond country, not without interest. The pass itself was a steep-walled, narrow, winding cañon, the cliffs rising so straight on each hand and so high that a man must throw back his head and gaze straight upward to see the blue of the sky; the ravine so narrow that time and time again he could hold out his arms and touch the granite cliffs upon each hand, and so crooked that more often than not a man could not see twenty feet ahead or behind.

And always the trail following the devious way of the pass was steep and sought the notch in the top of the cliff-wall. At times it was thick-strewn with crumbled fragments of the rocks above; at times, where it widened out to form a little pocket some twenty or fifty feet across, it was floored with sandy soil which caught and held the tracks of the cow or the horse which had passed this way. Sherrod saw this morning no signs of cattle, but saw readily in the sand in one of these pockets where it was damp from a small spring in the mountainside, the tracks which Bull Plummer's horse had left last night.

69

"The trail isn't travelled much, that's one thing," was Sherrod's sole comment.

For the only other signs at all clear were two weeks old and were the tracks left by Hawley when he had ridden furiously to the Bar Diamond from the Up and Down and a bad beating.

It was an hour after leaving the shore of the Upper Lake before Sherrod left the upclimbing trail behind him and rode out through the "notch" and to the top of the cliffs. He drew his panting horse to a standstill, turned in the saddle to look back along the way he had come, and a gasp of astonishment and admiration testified to his emotion. Below him, looking almost vertically down where he could drop a stone two thousand feet to its placid surface, was the lake. There were the falls, white in their spray, where the overflow of Upper Lake dropped down to make Lower Lake; there were those other falls where Lower Lake poured its water into the creek which went flashing its noisy way to the meadows of the Up and Down; there, half a dozen miles down the valley, were the bunkhouse and home corrals which he had left this morning, his own little tent showing brightly with its conspicuous white standing against the green of the scattering trees. And far, far to eastward were other glimpses of the valley and of the pine and fir-clad mountains lifting their august heads in lofty grandeur above it.

His eyes brightened as they swept the far-reaching panorama and came again to the rocky summits upon which he had stopped. It was all the Up and Down — it was all his! And it was glorious, wonderfully perfect.

70

He was still upon Up and Down property; he would ride across the uplands for two miles yet before he came to the dividing line between the two ranges. The soil upon which he now rode was infertile, unprofitable for the raising of cattle; hardly a twisted cedar could find root among the boulders and slabs of rock; only a few hardy little wild flowers with tough, intrepid roots and small delicate blossoms grew here. And yet even these upstanding cliffs had their purpose; they belonged to him and they were his fences.

"And now," said Sherrod to himself or to his horse or to the vast stillness shutting down about him, "where is Daybreak Spire?"

Everywhere about him the cliffs reached up into flinty peaks, their summits clear-cut against the sky, reaching upward thousands of dizzy feet. Had there been only one peak it would have been a simple matter; but there were scores of lofty spires. Which one?

"I was to prove that I wanted very much to see her, again, was I?" he mused. "And so you can bet she has picked out the highest, hardest to climb. Aha! There you are!"

Turning slowly, letting his eyes range along the tops of the mountains upon the far side of the valley, beyond the spot where he had seen her, he hit upon the one peak which he very promptly told himself should be Daybreak Spire.

It would catch the first glint of the rising sun before its neighbours, for it stood alone, rising abruptly from a rocky plateau, and its crest soared upward to a dizzy height. At the top it had the appearance of coming to a

71

needle-point; allowing for distance, Sherrod decided that there would be quite enough room up there for a man and a woman to sit comfortably.

He turned his horse southward again, across the barren tableland, and so came between ten and eleven o'clock to the fall of cliffs to the south, from the top of which he might look down into the lands of the Bar Diamond as he had already gazed down into the Up and Down.

Here he saw a valley very much like the one from which he had ridden, a little broader, a little shorter. The lakes of the Up and Down were missing here, but a swift stream of water, taking its source in countless mountain springs, sped through the range and looked like another Up and Down creek. Below him, in a wide meadow, only a mile or so from the head of the valley, were the Bar Diamond range buildings and corrals.

"A first-class outfit," thought Sherrod as he looked down upon the fertile meadows thick-stocked with browsing cattle and horses. "And all that stock belongs Plummer? Hm!"

He gave his horse a touch of the spur, found the down-leading trail, and stopped no more until he had come into the valley. Riding out of the mouth of the gorge where it opened into the Bar Diamond valley, he came suddenly upon an old corral, one side of which was a sheer wall of the cliffs, the other sides being roughly fashioned of logs and boulders.

At the base of the knoll upon which the corral stood were three men sitting their horses carelessly and watching the herd of cattle which, obviously, they had

72

just driven from the valley farther down to range in the cañons of the upper end. Sherrod saw that one of the men was his visitor of last night, and rode to meet him.

"Good morning," he called as the eyes of Plummer and of his two companions were directed curiously upon him.

There was no immediate response to his greeting. As he came closer he could see that Plummer's sharp eyes were dark and wrathful, that a little red flush had run up into the bronzed cheeks, and that the big right hand hanging at the man's side twitched nervously.

He saw, too, that the other men eyed him with open curiosity, and that they looked swiftly from him to each other and then to their foreman. And still none of them spoke.

Sherrod came on at a trot, his immaculately clad body jolting up and down as his horse carried him over the uneven ground, and drew rein close to Plummer.

"I don't know that I quite savvy your play," said the Bar Diamond man, his eyes never for an instant leaving Sherrod's smiling ones.

"What do you mean?" queried Sherrod.

"I mean," returned Plummer bluntly, "that your righthand man is a damn crook, an' that I've told him it's up to him to go for his gun an' go for it quick when we cross trails! So, I guess you an' me had better have things understood, too."

"That's what I came for," Sherrod assured him pleasantly. "I didn't want you to think that Ross acted on my orders last night when he rode after you and made you give the money back."

Again the two men with Bull Plummer exchanged quick glances, again their eyes came to rest curiously upon their chief's face. Plummer's expression had not changed, save that his eyes were a little darker, the flush in his cheeks a trifle ruddier.

"If he hadn't come up on me unexpected an' from behind an' throwed his gun on me before I was thinking about a crooked deal," muttered Plummer sharply, "he wouldn't have rode back at all."

"He didn't tell me how he did it," answered Sherrod. "I didn't want to know. If he takes it upon himself again to interfere in my affairs, I'm going to let him go. My men have got to learn that, just as you own and manage the Bar Diamond, so do I own and manage the Up and Down. I rode over this morning, Mr. Plummer, to apologise for what has happened."

"Apologies don't buy much," snapped Plummer.

"And," went on Sherrod, "I wanted to return your money to you."

He drew from his pocket a heavy, bulging purse, poured a handful of glittering coins into his palm, and extended it to the Bar Diamond man.

The three men looked at him first in plainly expressed amazement, then in a quiet contempt scarcely less plain. Plummer's big hand came out swiftly and in a flash the coins went into his own pocket.

"You're square, Sherrod," he said slowly. "You're a damn square man. I'm glad to have you for a neighbour. Hawley," he said to the heavy-set man at his elbow, "you an' Smith haze them cattle a little fu'ther up in the cañons. By then it'll be dinner, an' after dinner we'll take a run down to the lower corrals."

Hawley and Smith touched their horses with the spur and raced off across the narrow end of the valley. Their eyes were hidden swiftly, but before they had gone fifty yards the laughter of one of the men floated back to Sherrod and Plummer. Plummer frowned, glanced at Sherrod, and then turned his own horse toward the Bar Diamond bunkhouse.

"It's pretty near dinner time, anyhow," he said carelessly. "We'll have time to unsaddle an' have a coupla drinks before the boys shows up."

"I'd like to," hesitated Sherrod. "And — you promised to give me a chance for my revenge, you know."

"Come on," cried Plummer. "I'm kinda busy to-day, but you been square with me, Sherrod! As soon's the boys go to work after dinner, me an' you'll set in for a nice little game."

"I'd certainly like to." Again Sherrod's voice came hesitatingly. "But I have a very great deal to do and — you see, Plummer, I am actually taking control of the Up and Down, and the ins and outs of the work aren't as simple as a man would think, are they? I'd certainly like to play you again and for a good big stake. But — no, I'm afraid we'll have to let it wait awhile."

"Well, you better come along an' have a drink anyhow. An' you'll want a bite to eat before you go back."

"I tell you what I'll do," Sherrod said at last. "I'll take a little ride with you down to your headquarters. I'd like to see how you have things arranged. And then really I must hurry back. Some other time, Plummer. Thanks just the same."

So side by side they rode down the valley the little way to the Bar Diamond bunkhouse, Sherrod looking with great interest at the land, the out-buildings, the corrals, the arrangement of everything. And then, with a swift glance at his watch and a smile and a shake of the head at Plummer's repeated invitation to get down and have a drink, he said "so long," and rode back toward the Up and Down.

Before Sherrod was out of sight, Hawley had ridden a sweating horse into the barn and, leaving the animal saddled, hastened to the bunkhouse.

"Well?" he demanded of Plummer.

Bull Plummer looked at him steadily a moment. And then, his hard face growing harder, his keen eyes brighter, he said bluntly:

"Get the boys ready, Hawley. There ain't no use wasting time with a chance like this. Get Tom an' Lofty down to the other end to-night where they won't be in the way; I ain't quite sure of them boys yet. An' we ain't going to take no chances."

"Hard Ross —" began Hawley, only to be cut short by Bull Plummer saying curtly:

"Hard Ross is due to take a trip right soon to a place they don't run cattle none! And it's a place folks don't come back from!"

CHAPTER
EIGHT

It was late afternoon when Sherrod rode back to the Up and Down bunkhouse. He found Hard Ross in the corrals saddling a fresh horse, about whose rebellious neck an unerring lasso had just settled. Ross looked up at him sharply, grunted, and went on jerking his latigo tight.

"It's nearly time to quit work, isn't it?" queried Sherrod, slipping awkwardly and stiffly from the saddle. "And you look as though you were just starting out."

"I am," said Hard Ross. "I got a big job an' a mighty pleasant job on my hands this trip!"

"Yes?" Sherrod was unsaddling but looked interested. "What is it?"

"It ain't range business," Ross told him shortly. "It's just my affairs, same as it's your affairs where you been riding all day."

Sherrod laughed.

"I told you what I was going to do. I rode over to the Bar Diamond to return Mr. Plummer's money."

"Which was a worse fool trick than losing it in the first place," snorted the disgusted foreman.

"I haven't asked your opinion, Ross," retorted Sherrod with dignity. He jerked off saddle and bridle, turned his horse loose in the corral, and then, his voice pleasant again, asked, "By the way, where's Daybreak Spire, Ross?"

"Daybreak what?" Ross looked at him, frowning. "I don't know. I've lived in this neck of the woods quite some time, pardner, an' I never heard of a man or a horse or a creek or an outfit called Daybreak anything."

"I rather supposed that most people wouldn't know it by that name," sighed Sherrod. "By the way, Ross, I saw a man named Hawley at the Bar Diamond to-day."

"You did, huh?" Ross made no other comment, although his eyes remained steady upon the nose-glasses.

"Yes. An unhandsome sort of chap. Say, what's the name of the people who live up by the Twin Lakes?"

"Madden," said Ross. He had finished with his cinch, jerked the stirrup down and swung up into the saddle.

"Who are they?"

"They're Madden, who some folks calls the Hermit an' some says is part crazy, an' his stepdaughter."

"What's her name, Ross?"

Again Ross looked at him sharply.

"Her name's Dawn." He noted Sherrod's start, and then, a quick smile played for a moment upon the foreman's stern features as he added, "That's pretty near the same thing as Daybreak, ain't it?"

"Where do you expect to find Hawley?" was Sherrod's next question. "Going to ride all the way over to the Bar Diamond?"

"Who said I was looking for Hawley?"

"I did. It's just two weeks since I came to the Up and Down, and that means that it is just two weeks since you had trouble with Hawley."

"It wasn't any trouble," snapped Ross.

"And you gave him two weeks to bring Silver Slippers back to you. What made you think he stole her, Ross?"

"It's getting late," was the noncommittal answer. "It'll be dark up at the other end when I get there. So long."

"Wait a minute. I'm going with you."

Hard Ross made no attempt to hide his astonishment.

"You going with me!" he gasped. "Well, I'll be damned!" And then he muttered wonderingly, "What do you want to do that for?"

"Look here, Ross." Sherrod was polishing his nose-glasses with a deal of unnecessary energy. "You've been pretty decent to me this week. I didn't approve of what you did last night, but I appreciate the impulse that prompted you just the same. Now you're riding into danger, and I'm not going to let you go alone."

Hard Ross's big voice boomed out in a roar of hearty laughter. He wiped his eyes and finally gasped:

"You're going along to keep me from getting hurt, huh? Oh, Lord!"

"And besides," went on Sherrod hastily, "I was going that way anyhow. I just rode in to get something to eat to take something along for a bed, and to get a fresh horse. I'm going to climb to the top of the cliffs before sunup."

"What for?"

"Why," Sherrod answered smilingly, "let's say for the view! And to get a good appetite for breakfast. Now, rope me a horse, Ross, there's a good fellow. I'll have something to eat while you're getting him. I won't keep you a second."

He gave his order as if he had no doubt about its being obeyed and hurried off to the bunkhouse. Ross watched him a moment, then, loosening his coiled rope from his saddle strings, rode into the second corral, caught a tall roan that Sherrod had ridden once or twice, and tied it to a post. Then he headed his own horse out toward the upper end and rode on his spurs to get away from the man who wanted to protect him.

Ross soon left the main trail, and once he was riding where he felt Sherrod would not find him, he drew his horse down to a swift walk. He was looking for trouble to-night, he was riding straight into it with both eyes wide open, and he was too old a hand at a hard game to spend his horse's strength and speed before the time came for it. A fresh horse might mean a very great deal before the night was over.

A fresh horse might mean a live man in the morning, whereas a jaded one might mean a dead man to-night. Hard Ross, riding slowly through the ever-thickening dusk under the trees, drew his hat low over his eyes and shifted his gun from his hip pocket to the waistband of his trousers.

Then he made a cigarette, dropped the reins upon a well-trained cow pony's neck, and rode on thoughtfully. And Sherrod did not enter those thoughts.

80

"It's two weeks to-day," he said to himself with the first deeply inhaled draw at his cigarette. "Hawley'll be remembering that. He'll know I wasn't joking when I gave him just two weeks to bring Silver Slippers back. I'd have thought he'd have sense enough to do it. He'll be looking for me."

Here in these steep-walled cañons darkness came swift upon the heels of the sunset. Before Hard Ross had come to the steep climb from the floor of the valley to the level of the Lower Lake it was pitch black about him, his trail all but lost to the eyes in the inky emptiness beneath him. And when he made the ascent he did it warily.

It was quite within the bounds of possibility that Hawley had decided to save him the long ride to the Bar Diamond; Hawley might have ridden to meet him, might be waiting for him at any turn of the narrow trail. And Hard Ross, of a great mind to kill Hawley and of little mind to have Hawley kill him, slipped silently from the saddle and, holding an end of his horse's tie-rope, let the animal go on up the steep way ahead of him. And so he came to the top, and it was very still and very dark about him, and there was no sign that another man was within miles of him.

"A man that'll steal stock is a sneak," meditated Hard Ross when once more he sat still in the saddle before moving on again. "He's bound to be. An' it's a sneak's way to hide behind a tree an' shoot you out'n the dark. You ain't far off, Hawley."

Again he rode on cautiously, slowly, turning out of the well-beaten way many a time to ride upon a grassy bit of ground where his horse's shod hoofs struck no chance spark and fell silently. So he passed the first lake, came abreast of the second, and saw the black mouth of the pass opening before him.

And then, for the first time, he heard a sound which was not a part of the harmony of the night noises of the wilderness.

Instinctively, before even trying to catalogue the sound, he jerked his horse to a standstill and slipped from the saddle, his hand going to the revolver in his waistband. The noise came from just there, a little to the left, a little in front of him. It was just such a place as Hawley would choose.

Someone was walking toward him, the soft footfall cracking the dry twigs which lay in the grass. He waited, his stern eyes boring into the wall of the darkness. He saw a spurt of flame, and the gun came leaping out of his belt, ready. But the flame was only a match.

The match went its short journey to the ground, for a moment was lost to him, and then the larger, brighter flame of a leaping bonfire licked at the darkness as the fire ran through a pile of dry brushwood and gnawed at the rotten log thrown across it; the sudden, bright light made the mouth of the pass as clear as day. And Ross made out, and frowned at what he saw, that the individual who had lighted the fire and who now stood back a pace from it, was Dawn Madden.

"What's she doing that for?" was his quick, questioning thought.

He had been certain it was Hawley; now it was clear that it was the girl. But why had she set a fire here where its blaze made the mouth of the pass so bright that a man riding through it would be a target hard to miss for any other man who might be waiting for him?

"Madden made her do it!" was Ross's quick decision. "An' Bull Plummer made Madden make her do it! An' if I go on an' ride through, there's going to be powder burnt inside two minutes! They're a nest of thieves, an' they're sticking almighty close together for this play."

He waited a moment, listening, watching, undecided. If he rode on, there was no way open save through the pass; and if he rode into the pass . . .

He shrugged his broad shoulders and swung back up into the saddle. He had come this far, and he was not going to turn back. He had made Hawley a promise, and he was going to keep it. He gathered up his reins tight in his left hand, his right whipped out the revolver which he was so certain now of using in a moment, his spurs were drawn back a little to send his horse racing through the circle of light.

Then again a sound broke upon his straining ears, and he hesitated. When he made out what this new sound was he drove his spurs home and raced ahead. It was the sound of a horse's hoofs behind him, heralding the approach of Sherrod, coming to protect him!

Hard Ross heard the girl's startled exclamation as he shot by her and toward the mouth of the pass, and he

83

heard, too, a voice calling from just behind him, Sherrod's voice, and he saw everywhere about him a black wall of darkness rimming him in.

He was almost at the mouth of the pass, leaning low over his horse's neck and riding on his spurs, when he saw a quick spurt of red fire from the shadows in front of him, heard the reverberating crack of a revolver, and knew that Hawley was there, waiting for him. The bullet whizzed by him and sang its way through the night; he heard the pound of running hoofs behind him; he heard the girl cry out again; he saw the angry spit of fire again not twenty paces from him, and still riding furiously he threw up his gun and fired back.

"Stay with him, Ross! I'm coming!"

It was Sherrod's voice ringing clear, and Ross cursed aloud as he fired again into the darkness. He was almost through the circle of light now, but that light was growing brighter each second, leaping higher, reaching farther as the running flames licked at the dry fuel. Almost across the widening circle . . .

Then there was another spit of flame in front of him, not ten steps away now; and Hard Ross, seeking to fire back, felt his revolver slipping from a nerveless hand as a hot streak of pain stabbed through his shoulder like the pain of a burning sword-point driven deep into the shrinking flesh, and, cursing at his weakness, pitched forward and fell — fell, still in the widening circle of light, and lay trying to rise, trying to force his dimming eyes to penetrate that impenetrable wall of darkness.

"Stay with him, Ross old man! I'm coming!"

Again it was Sherrod's voice, and again Ross, weak and dizzy, cursed. If it were only Sunny Harper, or Little John, or Happy Day! If it were only any one of the boys who knew how to ride and how to shoot! If it were only anyone on earth but the biggest damn-fool tenderfoot he'd ever seen!

Hard Ross felt another tearing pain in his side as he lay there, knew that Hawley had shot him again — and then he would not believe that he saw the things which he did see. His eyes must be playing him tricks.

He saw Sherrod riding at a breakneck speed over the uneven ground, spurring straight on into the brightening circle of firelight. He saw Sherrod sitting very straight in the saddle and riding like a man who was as much at home on a horse as Hard Ross himself was. He saw that Sherrod's hands, both of them, were at his sides, one holding the reins, the other hanging loosely.

"The fool!" he muttered. "The pore damn fool!"

He saw Sherrod race by him, stooping a little from the saddle as he swept past, then straightening again Sherrod's hands were still at his sides. A loud-voiced shout, a shout in Hawley's unmistakable voice, called to him to stop. And still Sherrod rode on, and as he rode he laughed! And Hard Ross had never heard a laugh like that from any man before.

Again there was the red spit of fire from the gun in Hawley's hand. Then Sherrod's right hand, no longer hanging loose at his side, sped to his hip; there was the crack of his revolver before the echoes from Hawley's gun had died away. Sherrod fired once only, and jammed the gun back into its holster. He reined his horse about in the trail and rode back to Hard Ross.

"You fool!" cried Hard Ross. "He'll kill you!"

Sherrod swung down from the saddle and stooped over Hard Ross, his hands going quickly to the red stain which the firelight showed already upon the foreman's shirt.

"Not hurt bad, are you?" he asked anxiously.

"Good God!" cried Ross, trying to sit up and then sinking back, the blood pouring like water across his breast. "We're in the light — you damn fool, I tell you he'll get you!"

"He won't get anybody, Ross," returned Sherrod coolly. "Didn't you see me shoot?"

"*You* shoot? Don't make me laugh! You can't hit a tree!"

"I never missed a man yet, Ross. Now, you be quiet. You're pretty badly shot up. And," Sherrod added with a quiet sternness which puzzled Ross as much as anything else had puzzled him, the words coming in a voice which he could not recognize as Sherrod's, "remember that I'm running this outfit and that you take orders from me!"

Hard Ross said nothing. He began to wonder if already his mind was wandering. He could be sure of nothing. He felt his lax body gathered up gently, tenderly, in a pair of arms which were like steel; he felt his big bulk being lifted by this tenderfoot as if he had weighed fifty pounds instead of close to two hundred; he knew that he was carried a dozen steps and laid down at the edge of the trail where the firelight shone plainly and where there was a carpet of thick, lush grass.

And, though he listened and craned his neck, he heard no sound of running hoofs in the pass, no sound of a man running, saw no other flash of a gun. He looked up into Sherrod's face, wondering. He made out that Sherrod's nose-glasses were not in their accustomed place, and that in Sherrod's eyes there was a sternness, a grim, bleak anger which he found it hard to reconcile with the man he knew, the man he had knocked down on the first day he came to the Up and Down. And then a sudden great, suspicion broke like light into his brain, making him forget the pain in his tortured body. He gasped:

"Say! *Who are you?* What's your name?"

"Sherrod," Sherrod told him sharply. "Now don't go to —"

"Not *Jim* Sherrod? Not Jim Sherrod from the Painted Rock country. Not —"

"It's nobody's business where I'm from, is it?" said Sherrod quickly. "My name is Sherrod, and I'm your boss. That's enough!"

But it wasn't enough for Hard Ross. He put his hand behind him on the ground and forced his pain-racked body into a sitting posture, his eyes wide as they rested upon Sherrod s face. When finally he sank back it was with a stifled moan of mingled pain and wonder.

"You let me knock you down!" he muttered. "An' I didn't know how close I stood to dyin'. A damn sight closer than I am right now! I saw that trick of the gun

— an' Hawley ain't moved! *You're Fancy Jim Sherrod, that's who you are!* An' I thought you was a tenderfoot! Oh, hell!"

CHAPTER
NINE

For a moment the lithe, sinewy form of Sherrod bent over Hard Ross. Sherrod's voice, in a swift, stern whisper, spoke but a few words, and Hard Ross, half-fainting from shock and fast-running blood, nodded that he understood.

"I am playing this hand my way," was what Sherrod had said briefly. "Can you keep your mouth shut, Ross?"

Ross sank a little lower, his shoulders back against the ground now, his head whirling, his mind groping in a sort of dark. Fancy Jim Sherrod! It was Fancy Jim Sherrod! Fancy Jim from the Painted Rock country. A man whom he had judged a tenderfoot, a man whose name had travelled far across the range lands, until five hundred miles from the Painted Rock men knew of him, knew his way with a gun, knew that his draw was like lightning, that he had a way of firing one shot and jamming his revolver back into its holster before the smoke cleared! The man who, single-handed, had cleaned out the Luke Verilees gang with four shots fired, all Fancy Jim Sherrod's, and four men lying upon the floor of the dugout where he had come upon them red-handed. The man who was born to bucking horses and running steers and swishing ropes, and who had come to the Up and Down wearing a derby hat and nose-glasses, with a smudge of ink on his fingers!

Sherrod, busy over his foreman's wounds, seeking to see in the dancing firelight just where they were located, to judge what danger the mute red lips of the torn flesh were telling, striving to bandage and stop the rush of blood, heard Hard Ross muttering.

"You mustn't talk any more than you have to, Ross," he said gently. "Is it anything you've got to say?"

Ross nodded again. Fancy Jim Sherrod put his ear close down to the hot lips and heard the muttered words:

"Hawley ain't moved yet. He ain't goin' to move."

"No," returned Sherrod very quietly. "He isn't going to move, Ross."

"He must have rode a horse, Sherrod. Will you go and see?"

"If it's Silver Slippers?" Sherrod drew the swiftly improvised bandages tight and got to his feet. "You're going to live through this all right, Ross. It'll take a lot of killing to put you down for good. I'll go and see if he rode Silver Slippers."

Then, for the first time, Jim Sherrod saw Dawn Madden. She was standing just at the edge of the ever-widening circle of fire-light, her hands gripping each other with trembling fingers, her eyes wide with the horror of what she had seen.

"You here?" he cried.

"Tell me," her shaking voice floated to him. "Is he dead?"

"Ross? No. He'll live. He is —"

"No, no. The other man. Was it —"

"I think he is dead," he returned with grave sternness. "I hope that he is. It was Hawley. He set a trap for a man he was afraid of. He tricked him into the light and shot him down."

"Ask her — who built — the fire!" came Ross's voice in a weak fluttering half-whisper.

"You mean —"

There was accusation in Hard Ross's voice; Sherrod's eyes were suddenly steely with a cold glitter as they flashed upon the wide eyes of the girl.

"I — I —" she cried wildly. "Oh, my God! my God!"

And then, her voice ringing like a wail of despair, she threw her arms up high above her head, then brought her hands down so that they covered her white face — and then she was gone, the shimmer of her gown fluttering away from them until it was lost through the trees.

Fancy Jim Sherrod stared after her a moment, his eyes frowning, his lips hard-set. Then with a little grunt which told nothing, he swung upon his heel and strode into the mouth of the pass where Hawley lay.

He stopped a moment and looked down on the sprawling figure with hard, expressionless eyes. Hawley's gun lay just beyond the outstretched fingertips; the body was very still.

With swift strides he passed on and into the narrow, dark throat of the cañon. Once or twice he stopped, listening. The horse would not be far away. Almost immediately he heard the low jingle of bridle chain and went on quickly.

The horse stood in a sharp turn of the trail, its tie-rope dropped over the limb of a tree. He caught up the rope and led the animal back into the firelight. A little coughing grunt from Hard Ross told him that the foreman had been watching for him, watching mostly for the horse that he led. It was a rangy sorrel, not Silver Slippers.

"Never mind, Ross. We'll get your horse back for you yet. And we'll send the sorrel along the trail to the Bar Diamond as a sort of hint that we're coming."

He yanked off saddle and bridle for fear that they might hang the animal up on some snag of rock or tree, swung the horse about in the trail and struck it smartly upon the rump with the palm of his hand, sending it shying wildly about its master's body, snorting its terror and fleeing along the uptrail. Then he came back to Ross.

"You're done up too badly to make the trip back to the bunkhouse, old fellow," he said gently. "I'm going to take you in here. You'll spend the night with the Maddens and if you're in shape we'll get you home to-morrow."

The last bit of Hard Ross's iron strength had left him, and he was lying back, his eyes closed, his face dead white. Sherrod stooped, slipped his hands under the broad shoulders and then straightened up abruptly, swinging about at the sound of a footstep almost at his side.

A man — he told himself that this was Mr. Madden, Dawn's stepfather — was almost at his elbow. With a distinct feeling of curiosity, he stared into the man's face. And there came to him an instinctive sense of distrust and dislike when he looked upon it for the first time.

It was the face of a man of the cities, pale, looking colourless in the quivering firelight, the complexion of a man who sees little of the outdoors, the pallor an unhealthy whiteness. The features were fine, even delicate, the forehead high, the eyes deep-set and brilliantly black. Against the finely chiselled lines of the lips and nostrils the heavy jet-black eyebrows were strangely incongruous. The man himself seemed out of place here under the steep ruggedness of the cliffs, and his costume — he wore a dark dressing gown which fell almost to his heels and a pair of slippers — accentuated the already marked incongruity.

"I'm Mr. Madden," he said sharply. "I heard you speak my name. What's been happening here?"

"This man is badly hurt," Sherrod answered slowly. "He has a couple of bullet holes through him, and —"

"I heard the firing. Who is he?" demanded Madden with the same sharp tone that hinted at suspicion.

"He is Hard Ross, the Up and Down foreman."

"Who shot him? You?"

"No. A man named Hawley."

"Where's Hawley then?"

"Back there," Sherrod told him a bit impatiently, "in the trail."

"What's he staying there for? Why doesn't he come on or run for it?"

"For the same reason that Ross doesn't move," said Sherrod shortly. "And as I said a moment ago, Ross is badly hurt. I want to bring him inside. When I mentioned your name —"

"You can't bring him into my house," snapped Madden. "I haven't any desire to get mixed up in this brawl!"

"You don't mean," returned Sherrod, his words coming very slowly, each word marked by a great lack of expression, "that you refuse to let this man be taken into your house?"

"That is exactly what I do mean," Madden answered him coolly. "This is none of my affair; I refuse to have anything to do with a drunken brawl."

"It was not a drunken brawl, Mr. Madden," Sherrod said very quietly. "I think you know that. It was a sober enough quarrel, God knows. Just a white man shot down by a crook."

"Who's the white man? Who's the crook?" cried Madden, a little of his coldness gone. "What do I know about it? I knew Hawley. He was a good, steady man. I don't know you fellows, and I don't want to."

He swung upon his heel, stepping back into the shadows. Sherrod called to him.

"Wait! I tell you that Ross is badly hurt! He needs care. If he lies out here in the night, it is going to kill him; if I try to carry him five miles back to the bunkhouse, it is going to kill him. You've got to let me bring him in where I can do what I can for him!"

94

"I'll do nothing of the sort." Madden's voice was curt, its tone final. "If he dies, it isn't my doing."

Sherrod didn't answer. He turned abruptly and again bent over Hard Ross.

"Can you get your arms around my neck?" he asked gently. "Try to help, Ross. Hold on if you can. I may have to use my right hand."

Ross lifted his two big hands weakly and clasped them about Sherrod's neck. Sherrod straightened up, lifting his foreman in his arms, and remembering the landmarks which he had seen this morning, the great square block of granite, the log bridge, the stream escaping from between the two big boulders, made his way carefully, slowly toward the shelter which had been refused him.

"You're going to take me in anyhow?" whispered Ross faintly.

"Don't talk," answered Sherrod quietly.

So they came to the log, and Sherrod carried his burden across it, and to the entrance between the two boulders. But Madden had been before him, and a massive door of thick, rough-hewn slabs had been drawn shut, fastened with a heavy lock.

He laid Ross down upon a level, grassy spot near the door and called out loudly:

"Stand aside in there! I'm going to shoot the lock off!"

He waited a moment; no answer came, there was no sound from inside. He placed the muzzle of his gun close to the lock, and the roar of the explosion echoed loudly through the still cañons. He put his shoulder to the door, threw his weight against the thick panels, and the door flew wide open.

He took Ross up into his arms again and moved across the threshold. Stepping from the dimness of the forest, he came suddenly into a brilliantly illuminated interior. A lamp with mirror-like reflector swung from a beam high above his head, other lamps were bracketed against the walls. Small wonder the place was as bright as day — electric lights!

That at first startled him. Then he realized how simple a matter it could be here, where the water-power of leaping falls was unlimited, for a man to install his own electric lighting plant, and be profligate with illumination here where profligacy would be cheap enough. But still, as he moved on, his eyes alert and watchful, he marvelled at the things which he saw.

He was in a wide, high room, whose walls and ceiling were of beautifully veined, highly polished woods, whose floor was hardwood, glistening and bare save for the great bearskins scattered across it. There were a couple of couches smothered under soft cushions, two or three deep leather chairs, a couple of long tables, and little other furniture.

He barely noted a rare painting upon one wall, a piece of exquisite statuary upon a pedestal, the silken curtains draping a wide door at the end of the room. He had found a place to lay Hard Ross; that was the main thing now. So he stepped to the nearest couch and placed the wounded man upon the cushions.

"I suppose that you realize that you are breaking the law, Mr. Sherrod?"

It was Madden's voice, and Madden was standing there across the room, his hand upon the curtains he had swept aside from the doorway. His pale face was distorted by a black rage; his eyes burned malevolently; his lips writhed over the low-spoken words.

"I realize that the only law which counts at a time like this is the law of humanity, Mr. Madden," Sherrod returned sternly.

He again gave his attention to Ross, stripping away the clothing from the limp, blood-stained bulk of the man's upper body, seeking again to stop the flow of blood. But he did not turn his back upon his unwilling host.

To Sherrod, who had known many men of many types, who had lived his life as he had found it where life runs its way untrammelled, where the expected is often enough the unexpected, this attitude of Madden's was beyond comprehension. For one man to deny shelter to another who was in the sorest need, as Hard Ross so plainly was, called either for some great, compelling motive or for a reptilian nature such as Sherrod had never met. He had known hard men, cruel men, bad men and good; he had never yet known a man, good or bad, who would deny shelter and aid to a man shot down at his front door.

While working over Hard Ross, he turned his eyes again and again to the white-faced man watching him in stony silence. He saw the look in Madden's eyes, saw while he could not interpret it. He saw Madden's hands nervously busied with whatever they chanced to touch, the quick fingers turning and twisting at the tassel of the cord about his dressing gown, twitching at the silk curtains against which his tall, meagre frame was still outlined, running aimlessly across the close-shaven chin.

He saw that the man was anxious, worried, upon the verge of some nervous, querulous, explosive speech. And yet as the moments ran by Madden did not stir from his place, his eyes did not leave the two figures at the couch, and he did not speak.

"The man is afraid of something," Sherrod told himself. "If there's any one principal emotion he's struggling with, it's fear! Fear of what?"

He shrugged his shoulders and did not try to answer his own question. It was beyond him. Perhaps future events would show.

"What about the man Hawley?" At last Madden did break the silence. Sherrod had been working ten minutes over the still form of his foreman and now straightened up. "Are you going to leave him out there for the coyotes?"

The question coldly spoken; there was no hint of emotion in the man's even tones.

"I am going out to look to him in a moment," Sherrod returned as coldly. "I expect to find that he is dead. With your permission, I'll bring the body into the house."

"And without my permission?"

"Yes. I'll bring him in anyway."

Madden's lips curled back, for a second showing his small white teeth. Then he, too, shrugged.

98

"Do as you please," he snapped. "You'll spatter blood over everything I own, I suppose. I wish the whole crowd of you was in hell."

He turned with the last word, the silk curtains dropped back into place behind him, and he had gone.

"If you're going outside," said Hard Ross tremulously, "slip my gun in my hand, Sherrod. I don't trust that man none!"

"My God!" cried Sherrod. "You don't think he'd murder you, do you?"

"Slip my gun in my hand, anyway," said Ross.

Sherrod placed Ross's revolver on the couch so that Ross's lax fingers rested on the butt of it. He had seen men badly hurt before now; he felt that all that Hard Ross needed, a hard man in that great physique of him, a hard man to die, was rest now, care afterward. Sherrod went outside. He came to the mouth of the pass where the body of Hawley lay as he had left it. And there, white and wide-eyed, he found Dawn Madden.

"He is dead," she said colourlessly.

She had been crouching down over the quiet body; now she rose slowly and stood rigid and straight, the look of one stricken upon her drawn white face.

"I don't think I ever knew until now just what it means to be dead," she went on in that strange, even voice. "I keep thinking, over and over, what he was just a few minutes ago — and what he is now."

Suddenly her rigid tenseness broke under a terrible shivering which shook her body piteously.

"And — my God! It is I who am to blame for this!" she cried wildly.

Sherrod for the moment chose to ignore that it had been her hands which had lighted the fire which had so nearly brought Ross to his death, seeing in her only a girl torn with the violence of horror and grief, a girl too young, too tender to withstand the shock of the night's brutal tragedy.

"Dawn," he said very gently, "you must not talk like that. And you must not think like that. Listen to me, Dawn, poor little tortured Dawn Madden."

Gently he had laid a hand upon her shaking shoulder; instinctively he felt that now was a time when a spoken word might speak less eloquently to a cringing soul than the quiet touch of a sympathetic hand. But she jerked back from him, drawing away step by step until the body of Hawley lay between them.

"I lighted the fire; you fired the shot," she said stonily. "We are two murderers, you and I."

"You are a poor little girl who should never have seen a sight like this," he said softly. "But you must try —"

"Tell me," she cried fiercely, without heeding him, "is Hard Ross dead, too? Is he going to die?"

Before he could answer he saw her outflung hand drop limply to her side, saw her body seem to relax, beginning to sway, and thought that she was going to fall. In an instant he was at her side, his arms had crept about her, and he was holding her tight, seeking to comfort her, longing for some way in which he might physically interpose his body between hers and all trouble in the world.

But again her trembling body stiffened, and she thrust him away from her.

100

"Don't let him die," she said dully. "You mustn' let him die." Swiftly her two hands shot out, gripping his shoulders convulsively. "Listen: if Ross dies it means that to-night I have caused the deaths of two men."

And then, in a flash, she was gone from him. Gone, not into the house, but down to the lake side, beyond the upper shore, and on into the wilderness of great trees and giant cliffs. And Jim Sherrod, watching her until the darkness hid her, felt his heart going out of him after her.

CHAPTER
TEN

Already the silver globe of the moon had floated high above the cliffs; its soft radiance flooded the surfaces of the lakes and interwove intricate patterns of light with grotesque shadows.

It was a night of rare loveliness and serenity, and yet to Sherrod it breathed a vague, impalpable, nameless threat.

It seemed to him that the stillness about him was the hush of death, the quiet of expectancy, a listening of all Nature for the something which was going to happen before the moon had gone its journey through the blue arch and the sun had come. True, he had told himself that the misgivings which had inspired Hard Ross to ask that his gun be placed where his fingers could curve about the grip were born of the fancies of a fevered brain. And yet he sensed the sweeping onward of other forces to some end which he could not see, and he went swiftly, a little anxiously, about the task before him. He wanted it over and done with; he wanted to be back there with Hard Ross, watchful over his wounded foreman.

The moon ended his brief hesitation for him. A long, ghostly finger of light, quivering through the swaying grass, trembling across the Upper Lake, pointed to the dugout against the cliffs on the farther side. He could put Hawley in the cabin, close the door, pile rocks against it, and there leave the body until Plummer's men could come for it.

He strode rapidly about the head of the lake and to the dugout door. He could see in the bright moonlight that the rough building was, as Dawn had told him, very old. The rotting logs looked as if a man could jam his fist through them. The door, though of heavy oak slabs, looked as flimsy as the rest of the shack.

He put his hand against the door and pushed against it, at first gently, then firmly. The door did not budge. That surprised him a little, though at first he paid no great attention to it. He put his. shoulder against it and threw his weight upon the old, worm-eaten panels, expecting to lift the thing off its rusted hinges. Still it did not give a fraction of an inch.

"That's funny," muttered Sherrod.

He looked closer. Then he saw at the side of the door and in the shadow of the square doorpost, a heavy padlock.

"And that's stranger yet," he told himself irritably, "to put a lock like that on the door of a building whose walls a good puff of wind would blow down!"

Of no mind to shoot this lock off as he had done another already to-night, he left the door and went to the side of the dugout. He found a log, a part of the wall, that was lying loosely in its place, its surface rotten, and with a quick jerk pulled it away so that he could slip his hand through the opening he had made.

And as he did so there came swift warning to him that he was being watched, and that here, in the moonlight, was no place to loiter.

A rifle-shot cracked sharply through the silence, and a bullet whizzing by his head imbedded itself in the wall. He leaped backward into the shadow, but not before he had realized that the shot had been fired from the strange house where he had left Hard Ross; not until he had felt what lay behind the wall of rotting logs. And of the two things the rifle bullet puzzled him far less.

For his fingers, bursting through the dead wood, had come against a solid wall, a wall which he knew was of sheet iron. This old shack, looking so flimsy a shell for the wind to blow down, was in reality like a steel safe, walls and door and roof no doubt being lined within by a substance which would turn a bullet, defy an axe, yield only to something like dynamite or giant powder.

"Madden's storeroom!" muttered Sherrod as, drawn back into the shadows, his eyes went first to the little puff of smoke hanging ghostly in the pale light where someone — Madden, he felt sure — had fired at him, and then to the dugout before him. "Walls of sheet iron, one wall the granite cliff itself! What has the man got so precious that he hides it here? He shot to kill that time, too! I think, Mr. Madden," and his eyes were hard and stern as he drew still farther back to return in a wide curve to the dwelling, "I think you're going to have some questions to answer before very long."

Walking warily, slipping swiftly through the darkest shadows, he came back to the spot where Hawley lay.

104

He gathered up the quiet body in his arms and, stepping boldly into the light, now went swiftly to the broad entrance between the two big boulders.

He saw nothing, heard nothing of Madden or of anyone else who might have fired that shot at him; he came into the room where Hard Ross lay and placed his burden upon another couch at the far end of the room, out of Ross's sight.

"Sherrod!"

"Yes, Ross."

He went to Ross's side in answer to the whisper, and bent low over him.

"Don't talk if you can help it," he said gently. "You're going to be all right, but you need all the strength you've got."

"Yes, I know," panted Ross weakly. "But — I heard a rifle."

"That's all right. Someone took a potshot at me and missed."

"Madden," whispered the foreman. "Look out for him. I saw him run and get his rifle. The curtains were caught back."

"I thought so. It's all right, I tell you, Ross. I'll keep my eyes open."

"Make him come in here. Keep him where you can watch him. He's up to something crooked. I saw it in his eyes."

"The sooner they show their hands the better now," Sherrod snapped. "We're ready for them. And you, Ross, you just lie back and rest. I want you to hurry up and get back into shape. You're the best man I've got, and I'm going to need you before this thing is over."

A hard smile tightened the foreman's white lips. For a little while he lay very still, scarcely seeming to breathe, his fingers lying relaxed upon the grip of the revolver at his side. And then, his eyes coming back from the ceiling and resting upon Sherrod's, he whispered:

"Send for the rest of the boys; we'll need 'em in the morning. Just start my horse home; he'll go. The boys'll see him in the corrals first thing in the morning, an' —"

"Yes," interrupted Sherrod thoughtfully. "I'll do that."

In a corner of the room he found a writing table. He wrote a short note in pencil to fasten to the horn of the saddle, explaining that Ross was hurt, that he and Ross were at Madden's, and ordering Sunny Harper and Little John to come right away and to bring some sort of stretcher with them and a wagon as near the lake as they could; they were to rush a man to White Rock for a doctor.

Then once more he left the room, found Ross's horse and his own where they had been left in the trail, started his foreman's saddle animal on the downtrail as he had started Hawley's on the uptrail, only without removing the saddle, to which he tied the note, tethered his roan to browse during the night, and came back quickly. He saw nothing of Madden, heard nothing of him.

"Now, Ross," he said when he had come in and closed the outside door, "I want you to rest absolutely, to hold what strength hasn't run out of you. I won't leave you a second until the boys come. To-morrow we'll have a doctor out from White Rock. You'll want a drink of water now; I'll scare up some whisky or coffee and shoot that into you pretty soon. Now shut your eyes, shut your mouth, and rest."

Somehow the night dragged through. Hard Ross, all that his name implied, lay very still through the long hours, breathing heavily, with never a groan, never a complaint to tell that he suffered all that a man must suffer with two bullet holes through his body. Again and again he turned his eyes to Sherrod, asking mutely for a drink of water; many times during the night Sherrod moved him a little upon his cushions, trying to make him more comfortable.

Few words were spoken, and yet before the sun came up the two men knew each other as two men may not come to do through years of acquaintanceship. Essentially different personalities, they were essentially alike in many things which counted.

Sherrod, pacing back and forth or sitting quietly watching his patient through the still night, found much to ponder upon.

Dawn Madden had lighted the fire which had so nearly ended all things temporal for Hard Ross. Why? It was hard to believe that she had done so for the one purpose which seemed obvious; she could not have done the thing so that Hawley, in hiding, could shoot down the man whom he knew to be looking for him.

Then, where was she now. He had seen her, wild with the horror of the scenes which she had witnessed, running from the spot where men's blood had soaked into the ground, running from him, running into the heart of the brooding forests. Where had she gone?

He was sure that she had not come in again. He listened again and again, his ears caught by some chance sound without, the moving of a bird in the branches above, the snapping of a twig, thinking that at last she had come back. But not once did he hear her step within the house.

He heard Madden — it was a man's footfall, it must be Madden — moving through a room at the back. He had heard something set down upon the floor, and he guessed that it was a rifle butt. Then there had been silence; he had not again heard Madden, he had not seen him.

So his thoughts, roving back and forth, came again to the puzzle of a shack with rotting walls lined within with sheet iron. What was it for, what was this thing which Madden hid there, so precious that it called for the protection of such walls, for the secrecy which the false walls of rotting logs insured? He had seen a restlessness, a nervousness, an anxiety, almost a positive fear in Madden's eyes. Did the strange log shack have something to do with it?

Sunny Harper and Little John, riding on their spurs, their eyes hard and menacing, their horses' hides dripping with sweat, dashed up to the Madden place a little after midnight, flung themselves from their saddles, and with little enough ceremony threw open the door and came in. Their stern eyes found out

Sherrod sitting with his chair tilted back against the wall in a corner, found the still body of Hawley, and went to the darkened corner where Hard Ross lay upon his couch.

To Harper and Little John, Sherrod was still the tenderfoot and not to be considered after a quick, curt nod in his general direction. They went straight to Ross's side, bending solicitously over him.

"Hurt bad, Ross?" questioned Sunny Harper, his hat gripped tight in the strong fingers of both hands, his voice unbelievably soft.

Ross's head moved a little back and forth among his cushions, negatively.

"Hawley done it?"

"Yes."

"An' you got Hawley?"

Hard Ross hesitated. He was to "keep his mouth shut." Such were his orders from a man he was no longer ashamed to take orders from. His eyes, uncertain, went to where Sherrod sat.

Sherrod, seeing, got quietly to his feet and came to the couch.

"Does it hurt you much to talk, Ross?" he asked.

"No," the foreman answered. And then, with his grim smile, "It hurts more to keep my mouth shut!"

"Then talk," said Sherrod bluntly. "Harper and Little John know how to put a double hitch in their tongues, don't they?"

"They sure do! You boys prop me up a little. I'm getting — tired laying down on my back. That's good."

He sat a moment, breathing hard, while Harper and Little John watched him curiously.

And then, abruptly:

"Sherrod nailed Hawley," he said. "He come just in time. He's from the Painted Rock country — he's Fancy Jim Sherrod!"

Sunny Harper and Little John, their eyes widening, swung about as if startled by a pistol shot. And then:

"My God!" gasped Sunny Harper. "Fancy Jim Sherrod! An' us fools thought he was a tenderfoot!"

And Little John, stricken speechless, stood with mouth dropping open and eyes growing still wider.

"Now," said Fancy Jim Sherrod sharply, "you boys, let Ross alone. He needs all the rest there is. And I'll spin you a yarn. Things are about ripe, anyway. First, how did you happen to get here so quickly? We didn't look for you before morning."

"I heard his horse's saddle leather," said Sunny Harper, his eyes still full of wonder as they clung to the face of the new owner, who was supposed to be a tenderfoot fresh from the city, and who was a man who knew more about horses and crooked trails and six guns than any one of the old Up and Down outfit. "I was laying awake, sort of worried anyhow. I knowed it was two weeks, an' I knowed Ross had gone looking for Hawley.

"Then I heard a horse come trotting down to the corrals, an' it was awful still outside, an' I thought I heard the funny sort of a noise saddle leather makes, creaking. I guessed it was Ross come back. Then, when he didn't show, I got to wondering, an' I went outside.

His horse had come close to the bunkhouse, nosing after some barley spilt by the outhouse, an' I saw him an' found the note. An' me an' Little John didn't waste much time hitting the trail."

"I'm glad you didn't," returned Sherrod. "And now I want to tell you something. I bought this outfit from D. M. Hodges, and I took it over with both my eyes open. I've been looking for a place like this for five years, ever since I sold the Painted Rock. I knew that there was a drawback; I knew that the Up and Down and other ranges hereabouts have been losing stock steadily. But I got the range at my figure and — and," he added significantly, "I learned that Bull Plummer was running the outfit next door. It looked to me like a pretty simple thing."

"You knew Bull Plummer before?" demanded Sunny Harper.

"I had never seen him; fortunately he had never seen me. But he worked a game with all the earmarks of this one in Montana fifteen years ago. He got away with it, too; he didn't pull out until he had to, but he got out of the game on time and with his sack full. I guess he's been here most of the time since. Now, my game was simply this: I buy up the outfit and come to take charge. The news gets around that I'm a tenderfoot and pretty much a fool into the bargain. I let Plummer ride right into camp and skin me out of five hundred bucks, easy play, rotten simple tricks. What happens? You boys do the usual amount of talking, and the news rides!"

Sunny Harper and Little John hung their heads and blushed.

"It's all right!" cried Sherrod softly. "I played you to do it, and I'm glad you did. It boosted my game! The whole country, Bull Plummer included, takes me for a greenie and a simpleton. Now, what happens?"

"You mean," frowned Sunny Harper, his eyes sharp under his contracting brows, "that Bull Plummer's guard's down, that he'll see a chance for a raw play, that he'll make it without wasting no time, an' —"

"An' we'll nail him!" whispered Hard Ross. "Oh, hell! I wish I was up an' riding a horse!"

"Lie still, Ross," commanded Sherrod. "All you've got to do right now is to take care of yourself. And you boys, you just sit close and do what you can for Ross and keep your eyes open and your right hands, where you can find 'em. I'm going out for a little ride."

He swept up his hat from the chair where he had tossed it, came to Ross's side and stood for a moment looking down upon him with sympathetic eyes, and then went out swiftly and silently.

"So it's ol' Fancy Jim!" whispered Sunny Harper, his eyes bright, his voice shaking a little. "An' he's got ol' Bull Plummer jumping after the bait like a sucker with his mouth wide open an' his eyes shet! An' us fellers is about due to see a spell of high life real soon. Huh, Ross?"

Whereupon Hard Ross nodded and then lay back very still, determined to take Sherrod's advice, to get his strength back in time for the showdown.

Meanwhile Fancy Jim Sherrod, leaving the Madden place behind him, went to where he had left his horse, saddled again hastily and, mounting, rode away through the splotches of moonlight and pools of shadow. And he rode the trail which Dawn Madden had taken in her wild flight from the spot where the fire her own hands had made had cast its light over such a happening as she could never forget.

"She's out here somewhere," muttered Sherrod. "The thing is enough to drive a girl like her mad! And standing it all alone — it's too much for her."

He felt that there was a chance for him to find her — a slight chance, but then if fortune was with him he might come upon her. And there was now no reason for him to sit still in idleness when his whole being craved action.

He rode the way his eyes had followed her as long as she was in sight, saw that she must have taken a well-defined trail leading along the cliffs, turning so that it swung around in a half-circle toward the mountains behind Madden's home. As the trail wound so did it climb, a narrow foothold hanging precariously to the granite cliffs, at times slipping between two upthrust shafts of rock with barely room for a horse to pass through, at times clinging to the outer surface with sheer dizzy heights below and above.

He felt certain that she had gone this way; there seemed no other way open to her unless she had turned aside into the tangle of brush and chaos of tumbled boulders through which she could hardly have made her way in the uncertain light.

Yes, she would follow an open trail, the first open trail which her flying feet could find. Her spirit would

113

be driving her on, urging her to hasten away from a spot that was still full of terror for her, clamouring to her to run from the pools of inky darkness below, to seek the white light of the uplands. He was certain that he was going to find her.

And yet he stopped whenever there was a bit of sandy soil in the trail and a bit of moonlight, looking for her tracks.

And at last, high up above the floor of the valley, in a little gorge where the sandy floor was damp, he found the mark of her moccasins.

"Poor little frightened kid," he mutterd as he straightened up. And then, his words bespeaking the swift trend of his thought: "Damn that man Madden! Why does he have to drag her into the mess?"

Here in the gorge he left his horse securely tethered. From here he must go on on foot. The way was too narrow, too ill-defined, too steep, at times being a straight upward climb over a fallen boulder, for his horse to travel it. He came at last to what he had thought from below to be the top of the cliffs; here he stood for a moment, panting, his eyes sweeping the expanse of moonlit country.

About him were peaks innumerable where the cliffs were split into ragged rock formations looking like towers and mosques and cathedral spires, a sleeping white city upon a floor of white. For a fog had risen from the lakes and the creek, and lay in a great horizontal blanket shutting out the valley below, made snowy by the full moon above. The granite of the many-shaped peaks was white, the whole a strangely

114

ghostly vision-city, piled in mid-air by some weird race of giants.

He was standing upon a small, gently sloping plateau where a little soil had accumulated in the hollows, where many frail-looking, hardy-natured flowers grew. He turned slowly, bringing his eyes away from the fog covering the valley and, turning, he saw, a little farther to the north, a great steep-sided tower of rock lifting its crest like a lofty campanile five hundred feet above the benchland upon which he stood.

The moonlight touched the monumental peak, showed the black fissures in the greyish white of the stone, and outlined the summit against the star-set sky with rare, soft distinctness.

"Daybreak Spire!" he whispered. "She is up there — and I am going to keep tryst!"

And then because the night was very clear, the moon almost at the full, the night air like crystal, he saw her where she stood upon the very crest of Daybreak Spire, her slender body outlined against the sky, star-set. And it seemed to him that now more than ever she was like the spirit of the solitude; a glittering star, scintillating with its diamond lights, pulsing with its green and white and blue fires, seemed set in her hair, a flashing jewel to crown a white queen, the tribute of the night to a maiden of the dawn.

She seemed lonely up there, all alone, with the world shut off from her by the white vapours below, with all humanity lost to her in the stillness of the night. She seemed, in some way which he could not understand, to be in need of him. She seemed, in some way which

115

he could not grasp, to be calling to him. He was in the shadow of the base of the peak. Had she seen him?

He began climbing swiftly.

CHAPTER
ELEVEN

Had Jim Sherrod been in reality the tenderfoot which he had seemed to be when Dawn Madden invited him to find her upon Daybreak Spire, he would not have been able to keep the tryst lightly offered, seriously accepted. For there was but one way which a man might travel and come to the top of the high-lifted, dizzy pinnacle, and it was not a way readily hit upon unless a man knew his wilderness and its mountains.

The obvious path, promising everything, fulfilling nothing, showed invitingly as he came close up to the base of the peak. Had he followed it, as he would have done had he known nothing of the way of a seemingly plain mountain trail, he would have clambered halfway to the point he was working for and there found his trail coming to an end upon a little shelf of rock with a perpendicular cliff rising fifty baffling feet above him. He would have wasted time here; he would in the end have come back to the base; he would have lost much time here in seeking the right trail; and in the end, unless his luck were far greater than his knowledge of such matters, he would have found nothing.

Sherrod saw the plain trail, but he stopped to make a cigarette before he decided that what was the obvious way was not the right one.

Dawn had gone ahead of him; to the tenderfoot it would have been difficult to know just which way she had gone. But Sherrod, upon his hands and knees in the moonlight, saw that she had gone the obvious way.

There was not a broken twig there to mark where her foot had rested, not a faint imprint in the loose soil of a hollow, not a sign of a stripped branch where she would have reached out to the stunted chaparral bush to help herself over the one steep climb. And so he looked elsewhere and found the path she had taken.

She had clambered straight up the side of the cliff for ten feet, helping herself by the cracks in the rock, by the branches of a manzanita growing hardily in a crevice in the granite wall. There were a few fresh leaves at the bottom; there was her moccasin print in the soil at the foot of the shrub.

Sherrod climbed up swiftly when once he had found the signs he sought. And then he came upon a narrower, steeper, more broken trail, hardly more than a series of precarious footholds and handholds, that led its circuitous hazardous way to the topmost point of Daybreak Spire. After nearly half an hour's climb he came to her side.

"I have come before the appointed hour, Miss Madden," he said quietly. "But I had to talk with you."

She was standing as he had seen her from the tableland below, looking out into the night. She had not moved in all this time, he thought swiftly. She was unconscious of physical fatigue or discomfort; she was fighting her battle of the spirit to-night, he sensed vaguely, though he could not understand yet just what that battle was.

She turned to him slowly, quietly. The terror he had seen in her eyes down, there in the valley had not entirely gone yet; he knew that she had not yet shut out of them the sight of all she had witnessed in the firelit, narrow pass. But her manner was quiet, her features composed. Her face was very white; she did not know it, but Sherrod saw that she was very, very tired.

"I want to talk with you," he said again very gently. "I want you to sit down and listen to me."

She did not answer; she did not alter the fixity of her gaze bent upon him.

"You poor little kid," he murmured softly, "you're pretty well done up, and I don't think that you know it. Come, you're going to sit down and rest. If you don't relax a bit, you're going to pieces."

He laid his hand very gently upon her arm. She shook it off with a convulsive shudder. He felt that she was trembling.

Still saying nothing, she moved back from the edge of the cliff and to a slab of rock where with a long, shivery sigh she sat down. Sherrod, standing half a dozen feet from her, looked down into the eyes which were still turned upon him, saw that their expression had not changed.

"Hawley is dead," she said, her voice strangely steady.

"Yes. But you must not blame —"

"I know what I know," she went on in the same steady voice which somehow told more eloquently of an unutterable soul weariness than if it had been choked with tears or strident hysteria. "And Ross? Will he die, too?"

"No," he assured her, though far from sure himself. "Ross is going to get well. He's badly hurt, but men built like Ross can stand up under a whole lot of punishment."

"But Hawley is dead. And you — you killed him!"

The words were thoughtfully, quietly spoken; a slight contraction of her brows showing in the moonlight told how she was trying to realize clearly all that had happened, to understand everything, to seek to know just where right lay, just where wrong.

"Yes," he answered.

Now he understood why she had shuddered under the touch of his hand when he had sought to draw her back from the verge of the precipice. And to himself he said again:

"Poor little Dawn! It's a bad, bad mess for a sweet youngster like you to be drawn into."

"You are so conventionally polite!" she said with the first display of anything bordering on emotion in her voice. "It makes me wonder if you are quite human, if you realize just what has happened to-night — what part you have had in it."

"You mean that I have killed a man and am not hysterical over it? That instead of thinking of your comfort now I should be in all things primitive and violent and brutal? That a lot of ranting on my part

120

would fit in better with what has happened, and then that it would be easier for you to realize that the events of a night are real because they then would seem in harmony? Is that it?"

She shivered as if cold. And still she looked at him curiously.

"I think you have guessed what I feel," she said, her voice again dispassionate and steady. He could see her white hands clenching desperately as they clung to each other. "It is a horrible thing to kill a man — it seems almost more horrible for the man who has done a thing like that to be unmoved by an act so ghastly, so terrible!"

Sherrod made no answer. He had not forgotten; it was one of the things which a man would never forget. He was not unmoved. And yet all that he felt must lie locked up in his own breast; he would not regret, he would not let it sadden him. And yet an episode like to-night's was bound to make of him a sterner, harder man.

"I heard Ross call you Fancy Jim Sherrod," she said out of a short silence. "Who are you? Are you — are you that man?"

"Men have called me Fancy Jim Sherrod," he admitted slowly, reluctantly, where another man might have boasted. "I am from the Painted Rock country."

"Then you — you have killed other men! This was not the first time?"

"I have killed other men," he said gravely. Then, his voice sterner than she had guessed it could be, sterner than she had ever heard a man's voice until now he spoke up crisply in his own defence. He said, "I am not a gunfighter, Miss Madden. I am not a brawler. I do not seek quarrels. I have never drawn on any man in my life save in self-defence, or in the defence of another man, or of my rights. To-night — you saw it — you know that there was no other way."

"You fired to kill!" She paused a moment, staring at him with her piteously wide eyes. "I saw! You fired the one shot and jammed your revolver back into its holster without looking to see what had happened. You *knew* before you pressed the trigger that — that there would be no need to look!"

"Yes! And what if I had not fired to kill! Would Hard Ross be alive now? He was down; his gun had fallen from his hands; he had two bullets through his body; and Hawley was still shooting at a man lying on the ground and badly wounded! Was that any time for me to hang fire?"

For a long time she was silent. She was no longer looking at him, but into the infinity of the star-spangled skies. Then suddenly she did look straight into his eyes, again, and said in a suppressed voice:

"I suppose that you did right. I suppose that a man could do what you did, and still be a good man. And yet — Oh, God! I'd rather be dead than do what you have just done so calmly! I'd rather be dead than have you touch me!"

Then at last her head drooped into her hands, she shivered from the moonlit crown of her hair to her moccasined feet. And in a moment Sherrod could hear her sobs, could see the shaking of her body.

122

He waited patiently until the sobbing ceased, until the tortured body was still. And then when he spoke it was more gently then before.

"You don't understand all that a man may feel," he began. "There are times in a country like ours where a man has to take upon himself a very great responsibility, the greatest responsibility perhaps that a man can shoulder. He has to decide in a matter which concerns not himself alone but the whole social fabric. He has to make up his own mind in a crisis. Will he stand by his rights and stand by his friends; will he cave in when the test comes and prove himself all incompetent to cope with such conditions, not of his own making, which he is bound to run up against in a country like this? He has one swift fraction of a second to decide — and that brief moment measures him as man or mannikin. It would have been easier for me to have held back and let Hawley put his third bullet through Ross's brain. And yet —" for the first time he spoke with a flare of anger — "and yet you would rather be dead than have me lay my hand upon your arm!"

He did not look at her now, but his eyes went moodily to rest upon the bank of mist lying below them, shutting out the valley. During the slow minutes in which neither spoke, both dwelt with their own bitter thoughts. At last, seeking to draw her thoughts into a divergent channel, and because there was a point on which he wanted enlightenment, he asked abruptly:

"You made that brush fire, Miss Madden. Why?"

She started up, lifting her head, her eyes widening again.

"I —" She hesitated and stopped. He could see that her lips were tightly compressed.

"We shall not wait for the dawn here," was what she said hurriedly. She rose and stood looking down upon him, her eyes filled with doubt. "We are going down to the house. And —"

"And you will tell me there?" he asked when again she fell silent.

"I shall tell you there," she replied. "Or I shall say nothing to you and — and I shall not see you any more."

She left him, walking swiftly. He followed her, making no further attempt at speech with her.

He watched her, fearful more than once that her tired body was unable to cope with the exigencies of the dangerous trail, ready to reach out and snatch back her falling body if she slipped. And yet not once did he offer his hand as they travelled downward. For she would rather be dead than have him touch her!

When they came down to where Sherrod's tethered horse was waiting, the first faint light of the false dawn was shining about the crest of Daybreak Spire above them. They entered the area of dense, white mist, passed through it, two ghostly figures, and came at last to the lake. In a little while it would be sunup here.

They had not spoken once on the long downward trail. At the door through which Sherrod was to enter the house, she left him. She would go in at some door at the rear. There she spoke swiftly, as if she would have it over with.

"You will want to eat, I suppose! Come to me in the breakfast room in half an hour. I shall have something to tell you then — or I will never speak with you again."

With that she hurried away, around the corner of the house and out of sight, and Sherrod, entering, saw swiftly that during his absence something serious had happened.

Sunny Harper, standing over Ross's couch as Sherrod threw open the door, whirled suddenly and came forward, his face stern and hard, his eyes blazing.

"Plummer's put another one acrost on us!" he snapped angrily. "Right under our noses!"

"What is it?" demanded Sherrod.

"Mute Adams just rode up with the word. Him an' Little John is outside taking a look aroun'. You know that herd of beef steers we slapped into the Big Tree Meadow? They're gone, the whole fifty head!"

"And you think that Plummer —"

"Who else?"

"I'm glad," said Jim Sherrod very quietly. Sunny Harper stared incredulously. "Yes, I'm glad. We're going to get busy, Sunny. We're going to trail those steers. We're going to find them on the Bar Diamond, and it's going to be the last deal Bull Plummer puts across on this outfit!"

"They're the pick of the range, Sherrod." That was Hard Ross's voice. "They're worth a good eighty dollars a head. Over four thousan' dollars of stock gone — an' me flat on my back!"

"Ross," said Sherrod sternly, "you lie still and get well. I'm going to need you pretty soon. We needn't hope that one night will end this thing. Harper, go out and find Mute Adams and Little John. Send Little John on the jump back to the bunkhouse. I want all the boys here; I want 'em on the run and armed. They're to have breakfast before they start. Then you come back here and look out for Ross. Send Mute here too. I want to talk with him."

Hard Ross, his eyes filled with the bitterness within him, a bitterness bred from the consideration that now, with the time for action at hand, he was out of it, lay back with a little grunt. Sunny Harper sped away upon his errand. And Jim Sherrod, coming to Ross's side to ask how he had passed the night, heard from somewhere in the house, the low voice of Dawn, the sharp, angry tones of Madden.

"We'll have a doctor here before long, Ross," he said, trying to shut out of his ears the indistinct voices. "We'll leave you here until he comes. I'll leave one of the boys with you. Then we'll move you down to the bunkhouse if the doctor orders it, or we'll fix up a bed for you and move you into town if he advises that."

"You're going after Plummer this trip?" asked Ross.

"We're going to try and find out where those steers went. Why, their tracks won't be cold yet! And we're going to bring them back. And — yes, I think that we'll have to ride over to the Bar Diamond to get them."

Then Mute Adams came in, his steady eyes a trifle curious and showing a new respect as they rested upon the owner of the Up and Down.

126

"Tell me about those steers, Mute," commanded Sherrod crisply. "How did you learn about it so soon?"

Then Mute belied his name and spoke swiftly and to the point:

"After Sunny an' Little John pulled out, saying Ross was hurt bad, none of us fellows went back to sleep. We loafed aroun' an' had coffee an' just got res'less, wondering just what had happened. Me an' Happy Day finally got the hunch we'd ride on up this way an' see about things. We rode slow, talking about things, thinking maybe we'd meet you or Little John or Sunny Harper coming back. Sunny had said for us to stick at the bunkhouse until he sent word.

"Then we come into Big Tree Meadow an' I said to Happy, 'Them big steers'll be rolling in fat in another week, Hap.' An' Hap he nods an' says, 'Yep, in case somebody don't run the bunch off!' An' then he sorta laughs, not thinking what he's saying might of happened. It didn't seem nowise possible.

"An' then we come to the wide part of the meadow where we oughta see some of them steers, it's so bright with the moon, only we don't see anything! Hap looks at me an' I looks at Hap kinda funny. 'Shucks,' we says; 'they're right over yonder, under the cliffs.' So we mooches over an' we're riding a little mite faster now, too. The steers wasn't there, an' they wasn't nowhere. Tracks didn't tell much, seeing the meadow's full of tracks. But pretty soon, down by the crick we found tracks as did talk. There was shod horses' tracks, an' right on the south bank of the crick where there's mud an' long grass we come acrost a sign a man could of read even if there wasn't no moon.

"A man had crossed the crick there, driving half a dozen steers, an' his horse had fell, an' there's the prints of the horse's knees an' the stirrup where it cut into the mud. An' it was so fresh the water as had seeped into the place was all riled up an' muddy yet! An' nary a one of them fifty steers in sight! Me an' Hap didn't waste much time fogging on here after that."

"You did try to see which way the herd had gone, however?" asked Sherrod.

"Yes, we tried. But I tell you the meadow's all cut up too much to show signs in the night time. We got a pretty good guess there was five or six saddle horses, an' we got the guess the steers was crowded on the run acrost to the dark under the cliffs."

"The south cliffs?" Sherrod asked quickly.

"Yes, the south cliffs," Mute Adams nodded. "The side nex' the Bar Diamond. Close up there, you know, it's all rocky an' hard an' broken, the sorta ground as don't hold no tracks. An' there a man couldn't say if they went east toward the. Lower End or west toward the Upper End. So we come up here."

"What time do you think the thing happened?" asked Sherrod.

"I'd jedge about midnight. Not over four or five hours ago. An'," he burst out violently, "think of the nerve of it! A night of a full moon as bright as day!"

"Never mind, Adams," said Sherrod quietly. "Those steers were wild and stubborn and unruly. They won't get very far in four hours, not through these mountains.

128

They must have come up this way, skirted the lake on the other side, and turned southward through the pass. We'll find the tracks there; we'll find the cattle on the Bar Diamond! You boys be ready," he concluded just as Sunny Harper came back into the room. "That means, be ready for trouble!"

They nodded shortly.

"We been more or less expecting trouble as soon's we found out Ross was shot up," replied Sunny Harper.

"All right. Wait here. I'm going to try to scare up something to eat."

He had for the moment forgotten the indistinct voices coming to him from the deeper interior of the house. Now again he heard them, Madden's irritable voice expostulating, Dawn's tones hushed and troubled. And then there was an angry cry from Madden, a scream from the girl, and Sherrod calling back, to Mute Adams and Sunny Harper, "Stay with Ross!" ran to the silk curtains, flung them back, and with no more ado ran toward the rear of the house.

First came a spacious, high room which would have drawn his admiration had he had any time for such an emotion. Here was the spring, bubbling up clear and cool in a rock-rimmed basin, dancing across the stone floor in a little hollowed channel, to sink out of sight and run under the floor of the room he had left, to appear again outside in the stream with the log bridge across it. The big room was like some flowery patio in a tropical home, save that fifty feet from the floor, a roof shut out the sky, and glowing chandeliers made a soft light.

There were bearskin rugs everywhere, there were silken cushions, there was an exquisite bit of statuary in white marble beside a flower-edged, natural pool in which a few brilliantly speckled trout steered swiftly. There were wide, deep windows looking out through the trees and vines upon the outside wall; there was a broad, winding staircase of glistening hardwood leading thirty feet upward to a tiny balcony that was a riot of coloured blooms, where Sherrod's quick eyes espied couch, cushions, and a table, book-covered.

The voices were silent now. They had come from some room still farther back. He paused a moment, uncertain. There had been menace in that sharp cry of Madden's, there had been positive fear in the girl's. Where were they? Where was a door leading to them?

At last he saw a narrow door in the extreme left-hand corner of the room. He hurried to it, jerked it open, ran on into a long hallway, turned at the first sight of another door, and suddenly found himself in a roomy kitchen where a stove was burning briskly, where the smell of bacon and coffee filled his nostrils, and where a Japanese, a shrimp of a man — or scorpion? — with a look like nothing on earth but that of an opaque-eyed Jap — was cooking breakfast.

The Japanese looked at him and away to his tray of biscuits, his face showing neither surprise nor even a fleeting interest.

"Where are they?" demanded Sherrod. "Madden and Miss Dawn? Where are they?"

The Japanese looked at him again without interest, grunted, shook his head.

130

"Wouldn't know," he answered simply.

He knew well enough, and Sherrod knew that he knew. But he saw swiftly the futility of argument and, catching sight of another door, he passed hastily through the kitchen and into the breakfast room. The table was set, a snowy cloth and gleaming silver service giving a rare touch of richness and taste and a further dash of incongruity here in the heart of the wild. The room was empty.

Then, before he could step to the door leading into the larger dining room, he heard another door, somewhere still deeper in the house, which began to seem a vast spreading labyrinth — he heard another door close noisily, and presently a man's footsteps coming swiftly toward him. A moment later Madden, his face drawn and white, his eyes hard and keen with the lights dancing like little fires in them, came into the breakfast room.

"For a stranger, you make yourself very much at home, Mr. Sherrod," he said coolly. "May I ask what you want?"

"I want to see Miss Madden," retorted Sherrod as coolly, though his blood was running hot. "Where is she?"

"She has gone to her room, if it is any of your affair. She is tired out very naturally, and has gone to lie down."

"But" — Sherrod's disbelief stood high in his eyes — "she was to meet me at breakfast. She was to tell me —"

"Tell you what?" snapped Madden.

"The thing you didn't want her to tell!" returned Sherrod angrily. "The thing because of which you have shut her up somewhere. Stand aside, Madden! I am going to find her for myself!"

Madden making no answer, stood aside. But his eyes were harder, more full of menace than when he had come in. And besides there shone in them a swift gleam of satisfaction.

Sherrod, passing him, hastened through the empty rooms, calling.

CHAPTER
TWELVE

The sun had flared up over the steep cliffs and was pouring a stream of golden light down upon the lakes, drinking up the fog, ushering in a brilliant, cloudless day. A half-dozen men, grim in their silence, were riding a dim trail whose end might well bring to any man of them the end of all earthly trails. Fancy Jim Sherrod rode well to the front, his eyes the hard, bleak eyes of a man upon a relentless quest.

An hour ago he had gone his way through the great, many-roomed house calling. Finally he had his answer. Dawn Madden's voice, shaking as it came to him from behind a locked door, assured him that her stepfather had spoken the truth, that she had gone to her room, that she was lying down; that she had nothing to say to him.

"Go away!" she had cried to him, her voice of a sudden breaking passionately. "I have nothing to say to you. Go away!"

He had gone without a word spoken back to her. He had breakfasted in Madden's breakfast room, commanding the apelike Jap to bring his food and not once addressing Madden or being addressed by him. He had seen that Sunny Harper, Mute Adams, and Happy Day had had their breakfasts; he had seen that Hard Ross had had something carried to him; he had left Mute Adams to take care of the wounded man; and then the other boys had ridden up from the Up and Down bunkhouse.

Now, with them at his back, he was riding to the Bar Diamond. And of all the hard faces Fancy Jim Sherrod's was the hardest. He could not drag his mind entirely away from the girl who could tell him a great deal if she wished, and yet who had cried emphatically, "Go away! I have nothing to say to you. Go away!"

She could not bear to have him touch her; now it seemed that she could not bring herself to speak with him. Just because he had done a man's part when it had been thrust upon him, just because he had fired last night that shot which had come between Hard Ross and his death, because he had killed a man who was a crook and a coward, and who, hidden in the dark, was pumping his lead into a man fallen, lying wounded in the firelight — the firelight which Dawn Madden had made!

These gaunt-bodied, lean, hard-muscled, keen-eyed men to whom the dimmest trail was but a blurred printed page, who read the signs on the ground as a man in the city reads his newspaper, had waited in a cool patience until the sun was up, until the light was strong, and then they had gone out to decipher the legend the night had scrawled along the brink of the creek.

They saw where the herd of steers had grazed in the early evening, found where one of them here and there

134

had lain down after feeding, and knew from the deep imprints of knees and hoofs that they had been startled to their feet, and had been driven at a run from the meadow to the stony soil under south cliffs.

These were the cliffs which marked the natural fence between the Up and Down and the Bar Diamond. And here at their rock-strewn base there was nothing to show whether the herd had moved east or west. In that fact, of course, lay the reason that the rustlers had driven them here.

The Up and Down boys, ready as they were at the reading of blurred signs upon the dim trail, got down from their saddles and for an hour sought to find conclusive proof which way the missing herd had gone. And in the end they had only wasted their time and had found nothing, for the steers had ranged here for ten days now, and there were everywhere broken spears of grass, trampled weeds, that might have been trodden upon after midnight or before. There were the same signs running westward as there were to the east.

"It's no use, boys," said Sherrod at last. He swung up into his saddle and reined his horse around toward the Upper End. "They took their chances on doing the job on a moonlight night; that's the only chance they took. Somewhere they've hazed the stock on over into the Bar Diamond, headed for the railroad. We'd better move on."

"Then they went through the pass," grunted Sunny Harper. "We'll pick up the fresh trail there."

So they rode back to the lakes, around the shore, clinging close to the cliffs upon the south side, passed the cabin with its rotting log walls at which Sherrod gazed frowningly, and found the mouth of the pass.

"If they went this way," mused Sherrod, still riding silently in front of his silent cowboys, "we'll find the tracks plain enough in the first sandy-floored pocket."

So they passed from the sunlight into the shadows of the steep-sided cañon which connected the two rangelands, the horses now forced to drop one behind another, the eyes of all men seeking for the tracks of the stolen cattle.

At the first pocket, where there was a floor of moist sand, Sherrod drew rein. The sun was now glancing down into the pass, and there was no need of men getting down from their saddles. There had been no horse, no cow, to go this way since yesterday. That was plain. The only recent tracks were those left by Sherrod when he had ridden to and from the Bar Diamond, those left by Hawley's horse as it had borne its rider to the last meeting with Hard Ross and as it had raced homeward, riderless.

"There you are," grunted Sunny Harper, his face anything but sunny right now. "It's the same thing over and over again. The stock's gone, we know who took 'em — but were did they go?"

"There's some other pass through these cliffs!" retorted Sherrod sharply. "The cattle couldn't have been driven down the valley; we would have seen the tracks somewhere in the lower meadow. They couldn't have flown over the cliffs, could they? There's some other way!"

136

"There ain't any other way," answered Sunny Harper as positively. "Us boys would know about it."

"Then where are they?" snapped Sherrod irritably.

Sunny Harper lifted his broad shoulders.

"I dunno. Don't ask me. Ask Bull Plummer!"

On the word Sherrod shot his spurs home.

"Come on!" he cried. "We'll make an early call on Bull Plummer, anyway. And we'll find the trail on his side of the cliffs. We'll find the cattle there, too."

The thing had happened as Sherrod had planned it to happen, played it to happen, and he was puzzled. It had been his hope that when the news went out over the range country that a tenderfoot had come to assume charge of the management of the Up and Down, the men who had long been stealing cattle of the U & D brand would be tempted to a bold stroke, to just some such theft as the one committed last night. Then he would strike, swift and hard, and there would be the end to trouble.

The news had travelled forth as he had meant it to do, the bold stroke had been made, fifty head of cattle driven off in a night, a moonlight night! And those big running steers had left no trail behind them!

"There's some other pass," he kept telling himself, "some way the boys have missed. And we'll find every hoof of them on the Bar Diamond, at least we'll find their trail there."

But still he was troubled. He had been in the valley two weeks, he had ridden much up and down, he had kept his eyes open. And he had seen no single place where a herd like this could have been driven from the floor of this valley to a neighbouring range.

They rode swiftly and made no stop until they came into the Bar Diamond pastures at the upper end where the stone and log corral was. From here they could see the Bar Diamond bunkhouse, could see the smoke rising from the cook's stove. A man was standing in the doorway, another man was drinking at the spring just back of the building, two more were going down to the corral, evidently for their horses.

"It seems that they've just had breakfast," said Sherrod sharply. "Let's get down there in a hurry. I want to have a look at their horses before they saddle up."

Riding six men abreast, the Up and Down cowboys raced down upon the Bar Diamond outfit. The man in the doorway called something to another man within the. house; the two men going down to the corral and the man at the spring came with quick strides back to the bunkhouse.

"Suspicious cusses," grunted a man at Sherrod's side.

"Why shouldn't they be?" returned Sherrod. "Now, you boys keep your mouths shut and your eyes open. This is my game; I'm playing it my way. And if I play it like a fool, that's my business and I know what I'm about."

Bull Plummer, bull-throated, bare of arm, was in the doorway now, his great bulk taking up most of the narrow space, his big hands busy with the cigarette he was making. Not a word was spoken until the six riders

138

were close enough to him to see his eyes, eyes which were hard and watchful and told nothing.

"Good morning, Plummer." It was Sherrod speaking, as he reined in his horse, and the other Up and Down cowboys set their ponies up just behind him. "Seen anything of fifty steers wearing a U & D brand? I've lost that many since last sunset!"

Bull Plummer's eyes held steadily to the eyes of the theatrically dressed cowboy. He saw nothing in them but the expression which Sherrod wanted him to see, a bit of vexation at his loss. Then the Bar Diamond man's gaze shifted, running like lightning to the other stern faces, the faces of the men sitting silent, leaving the talking to their boss.

"I don't quite get you, pardner," Plummer said quietly after a brief pause. "You mean —"

"I mean," broke in Sherrod impatiently, "what I say! I've lost fifty head in one night, and that means close to four thousand dollars gone like that!" He snapped his white fingers, and the little sound cracked distinctly through the silence which dropped down over his words. "Have you seen them?"

Plummer, while Sherrod was speaking, had stepped just outside of the bunkhouse. His men, who had gone out already, were drawn close now, and their eyes were as watchful, as inscrutable as his own. Four more men came out after Plummer and stood silent by the door.

Already there was a strained atmosphere over the two groups of men, although no belligerent word had been spoken. Every man was ready for whatever might come next, the open accusation which might well lie back of the words Sherrod had spoken. And although there was not a gun in sight excepting the two heavy-calibre Colts swinging ostentatiously at Sherrod's hips, there was not a man of them who was not ready upon the instant to go for his gun. The men sitting in seeming carelessness in their saddles, the men lounging by the door, Bull Plummer rolling a cigarette with big, slow fingers — they were all alike alert.

"I ain't been riding range for the Up an' Down," said Plummer slowly. "I don't know why you come to me looking for your strays."

"That's just it!" cried Sherrod. "Are they strays? If they've just wandered off the range, I've got some one of my own men to fire for not attending to my business better. And if some thief has driven them off for me —"

"Go easy there, young feller!" cut in Plummer shortly. He had finished making his cigarette, it was held between thumb and finger of his left hand; his right hand was at his hip, with thumb hooked into his belt. "It sounds almost like you was making a pass it ain't healthy none to make to me! What are you driving at? Do you mean you're thinking I've stole your damn cow brutes?"

"I don't know what to think, do I?" retorted Sherrod. "My stock's gone. Where did it go? I'm not saying you had a hand in it, am I? But you might have seen the steers if they did wander off, or one of your men might have seen them. I don't want to stir up trouble."

Plummer's deep laugh cut him short again.

"I guess you better not try to stir up anything!" he snapped. "If any of you jaspers is looking for a fight,

140

you come the right place to get it, an' damn quick! You just say I had a hand in the thing, an' I'll slap the white face off'n you! Just the same," he sneered, "as Ross done the first day you showed up! You better hit the trail back to town little man. An' hit it while the trail's open."

"But look her, Plummer" — and Plummer's men smiled at the quick change in the tone so mollifying all of a sudden did it sound — "I'm trying to do what's right, am I not? If you'd lost a bunch like that, you'd be worried too, wouldn't you? I just wanted to ask you to have a look around."

"You've asked your fool question, an' you've got your answer," answered Plummer. "Now since you're here, go take your look aroun'. But if you bring them sheep-herders of your'n on my place again, I'm going to stick my men on 'em an' drive the last one of 'em off same's I'd drive off a pack of kyotes."

"I hope there's no harm done," began Sherrod placatingly. And then, surprising his own men as much as he surprised Plummer, he called sharply, "Come on, boys!" shot his spurs home and sent his horse racing for the stable.

He had watched his chance and taken it. It looked like the fool play he had suggested that they might expect from him, but Jim Sherrod knew very well what he was doing. He had waited until not a man of Plummer's outfit was within two hundred yards of the corral and barn, and then in a flash he had dashed out of their midst, had raced into the corral, flung himself from the saddle when the barn was between him and

141

the bunkhouse, and had run through the big wide double doors.

There were a dozen saddle horses in the corral and stable. He merely glanced at them, saw that their hides were dry with not a hair turned by a hard night's riding, and knew that if Plummer's men had run off his steers for him they had not ridden these horses. Then he had plunged into the barn and had been there a moment, had hurried out again and thrown himself into the saddle. Even his own men, hurrying after him in a storm of thudding hoofs, with the dust puffing up like smoke after them, had not guessed what he was about.

"Come on," he called to them as they came up to him and he spurred out of the corral. And then his voice dropped so that only Sunny Harper and Happy Day heard the words, "We're coming back again — soon!"

They wondered and followed reluctantly as he led the way back toward the Up and Down. He did not tell them what discovery he had made within the stable. It was merely that every saddle blanket on its peg was reeking wet with sweat.

CHAPTER
THIRTEEN

Nothing had been accomplished, everything was to be done, and yet the days went their swift blue way over the Up and Down cattle range with no single step taken on the road to the untangling of the puzzle which was perplexing Jim Sherrod. An incredible thing almost, a thing which any cattle man would have said before the act was a rank impossibility, had actually occurred: fifty big steers had gone in a single night, and there had been no sign left behind to show the way they had gone. At least no visible sign, no hint to tell the keen, eager eyes of the Up and Down cowboys just how the thing had happened.

"I ain't sure," Sunny Harper was led to say at last, "but that the up-to-date rus'ler uses a airplane an' takes a string of steers off as a chicken hawk lifts a squirrel."

These were days of silence in the bunkhouse, days of drawn brows and unspoken speculation. Hard Ross lay upon a bunk made for him by swift, kind hands, at night in the warmest end of the sleeping quarters, by day, when the sun shone, outside. The little doctor from White Rock had come, expressed himself with brief and profane emphasis concerning the iron body he was called upon to care for, grunted that a man like Ross didn't have to worry over anything less than a dozen bullets or a shotgun at close range, pocketed his fee, given his simple orders, and ridden away, not stopping to ask how his patient got hurt.

As he took his leave of Sherrod at the corral, answering the questions about the seriousness of Ross's injuries which Sherrod put to him, the little doctor with a sharp look in his eyes said quietly:

"I'll be back before long."

"You think that after all Ross —"

"Who said Ross? I noticed the general direction of the bullet holes in him," and he climbed into his cart. "Looks like they came from the south, the Bar Diamond way! There'll be more lead from the same direction, Mr. Sherrod! Giddap, Nig. We've got thirty miles ahead of us."

Yes, there would be more lead from the south, and Sherrod didn't care how soon. But first he must find those steers, find the broad trail which they must have left — if after all Sunny Harper wasn't right about the up-to-date methods of cattle thieves — and fix the guilt where it belonged.

As the days ran by and brought no answer to the riddle, as Hard Ross got at last to his feet and walked a few steps about the bunkhouse, Jim Sherrod felt in his heart a growing bitterness, a bitterness toward a woman. Dawn Madden knew something, guessed much more perhaps; and she had sent no word. She would rather be dead than have him lay his hand on her arm! And she lived on with Madden, who was as deep in the mud as was Plummer in the mire — or else she had a lot to explain.

Sherrod had ridden several times to the Upper End. He had seen the strange dwelling place in which Madden lived his strange, solitary, luxurious life; he felt that Dawn must have seen him on at least one or two of his rides, and he had caught no glimpse of her.

"Evidently she'd rather be dead than see me, speak with me," he told himself every bit as savagely as the thought warranted.

Bull Plummer had stolen the fifty steers; the wet saddle blankets told their story of a hard night's riding; the fresh horses in the corral told their lie and made certainty more certain. Then where was the vanished herd?

It was the old question, over and over and over.

"It's enough to make a man go bugs," snorted Hard Ross just about as early in his convalescence as he was able to snort once more with his old-time vigour. "It looked easy to Sherrod, an' he played it right, an' now what happens? Plummer's got his five hundred in cash he euchered him out of, he's got as fine a herd of beef cattle as a man ever swung a rope over, an' the low-lived thief has got Silver Slippers! It's enough to make a man just ride over an' murder him, just for fun and on general principles!"

Silence that agreed met Hard Ross's hard words. A very little thing would have been enough on a day like this to send a dozen lean, hard, wrathful cowpunchers swooping down upon the outfit which lay along their side, which took and defied and mocked.

145

Every time Jim Sherrod rode to the Upper End he saw, too, the dugout across the lake and frowned over it, wondering what part it played in the tangle of Madden's interests here. It was situated — Dawn had told him that — upon the Up and Down property, and therefore it was Sherrod's and he had a perfect right to storm the thing and tear its secret from it. But, though tempted when his angry mood was upon him, he hesitated to do that. It would look like spite, and he failed to see what would be gained from it save the petty satisfaction of having annoyed a man he didn't like.

But one day, the thought came to him swiftly that perhaps after all he could use this pawn in the game and force something from Madden's hand, could force Dawn Madden to speak.

He would do the thing which he did not want to do, he would call in that other law of sheriffs and courtrooms and long, meandering proceedings. He would trump up a charge against Madden; he would force Dawn into court; he would instruct his attorney to wring from her unwilling lips an account of her lighting the fire which so nearly shone upon the end of things for Hard Ross; and there might be a beginning, a something to show him the truth he sought.

With the thought upon him, he rode straight to Madden's place. Madden himself, pale, his face drawn and weary, his eyes sharp and suspicious and watchful, met him at the door.

"Mr. Madden," Sherrod said quietly, "I want a word with you if possible."

"On business, no doubt?" retorted Madden, standing in the doorway, making no move to come out or to have Sherrod pass in.

"On business."

"Pray then," said, "make it brief."

"I have lost cattle," Sherrod began.

Madden cut him short. "I haven't stolen them. I am not interested in your stock."

"But," went on Sherrod evenly, "you are interested. At least, you know something of them, of who took them."

"You are accusing me of complicity!" snapped Madden. "If that is all that you have to say —"

"It isn't all," Sherrod told him coolly. "It would be as well for you to listen to what I have to say."

"And that sounds like a threat!" Madden laughed a short, barely audible laugh which was scarcely more than a writhing back of the thin lips and a harsh grating from the throat.

"And I am not making any threats." Sherrod's words were still coolly spoken, although Sherrod's anger found it a natural thing to rush out against this man. "I know who has taken my stock and I'm not making any bones about it. It's Bull Plummer! And you know a great deal more than I do about Bull Plummer and his work. I want to ask you some questions, that's all. I want to know if that fire on the night Hawley shot Hard Ross, and I shot Hawley, was lighted by your orders."

"It was not," returned Madden.

"Miss Madden lighted it."

"Then hadn't you better ask Miss Madden about it?" Madden demanded sharply. "She is very much her own mistress, Mr. Sherrod."

"I shall ask her as soon as I can see her. Is she in this morning?"

"She is not in this morning." Madden's tones irritated him again, seeming to mock him. "And she will not be in this afternoon or this evening!"

"May I ask when she will be in? Where she is?"

"Yes, you may ask, and I'll answer. And it's the last question I will answer. She has gone away; she has been away a month. She will in all probability be away for a year!"

And ke slammed the door in Sherrod's face. There was the sound of a heavy bar being dropped into place, and Jim Sherrod went away, more puzzled than ever.

Dawn Madden had gone away, had gone shortly after that night when he had seen her upon Daybreak Spire, no doubt. Gone where? To the city, to the East — where? No one would know but Madden, and to ask Madden would be to ask the cliffs, standing tall and stony-faced about Madden's home.

"I might have known that she was gone," mused Sherrod. "It was the natural thing. Why should she stay in a country like this? Madden never did a more decent thing in his life than send her out of it!"

Musing, he turned away from the closed door and swung back up into the saddle. He had not said the things which he had come to say, and the reason did not lie alone in the fact that he had had the door slammed against him. It lay as well in the fact that

148

Dawn Madden was gone, and her going might make a difference.

He knew that once the law was called into this valley it would stay, and it might hamper the free swing of his own action. And he would fail in the thing he wanted, an explanation from Dawn Madden of the lighting of that fire.

As had happened so many times before, his questing, frowning eyes went across the lake and to the dugout. This morning in the bright sunlight it looked a flimsy thing which the breeze rippling the lake's surface might topple over. He wondered, as he always wondered when he saw it, what precious secret lay hidden within. And to-day, with a sudden impulse, he turned his horse from the main trail and rode around the head of the Upper Lake and to the cabin.

Madden had taken a shot at him the last time he came there; Madden would be watching him now. The man might shoot again, and in the daylight he might not miss his target by the couple of inches he had missed before. But in his present defiant mood Fancy Jim Sherrod felt like taking any chance which might lead to decisive action. He had loitered long enough.

He came to the cabin door and sat still in the saddle, looking upon the outer, crumbling log walls. And his eyes, very keen now under the low-drawn brim of his hat, watched, too, the Madden place, half expecting to see the nose of a rifle barrel.

And what he did see at the cabin itself was something which he might have seen a month ago if he had ridden here, or might have missed. A small, negligible thing, insignificant but given significance now because of its position and because of the groping for any point in the tangle, no matter how small, by the mind of the man who saw it.

A soiled bit of paper such as a man would ride over and not notice; a piece of notepaper that had once been white, now darkened by exposure and the night dews. It was showing in a crack between two horizontal logs of the west wall, folded, just a corner showing, looking as though it had been thrust outward through the chink by someone inside.

"A note for Madden!" was Sherrod's quick thought. "It's got something to do with this infernal mix-up — and I'm going to tamper with the mails!"

He glanced swiftly back toward the Madden house, from it to the paper. He could ride about the cabin, ride close to the wall, bend a little from the saddle, snatch the paper as he passed; and he did not think that Madden, were he looking, could see.

It might be nothing, but on the other hand it might be the first small hint he wanted; its position bespoke secrecy if it were a note and that suggested something hidden that he had sought to know. He did not look again behind him.

He touched his horse with the spur, swung to the side along the cabin wall, snatched the paper as he rode past, and, holding it close to his thigh, hidden in his palm, turned along the cliffs toward the Up and Down headquarters.

It was not until he had passed out of sight from the eyes which he was sure were watching him, hidden by

150

hill and forest growth, that he looked at the soiled scrap of paper. And his heart leaped, grew still, and his face went white. It was a note; it was written to him, Jim Sherrod; it was from Dawn Madden!

His name was at the top of the hastily scrawled sheet. The writing was in lead pencil. It was already dimmed, but fortunately the folding of the sheet of paper bringing the note inside, had saved these words to him:

To be given to Mr. Jim Sherrod:
Plummer was with me. He had me by the throat. He said he'd kill me, kill you and Ross if I didn't tell you to go away. I was going to tell you all I know. Now — I'm afraid! They are going to get me out of the way — I don't know where. There is a cave, somewhere, 'way up on the cliffs. The Jap, Koto, is to bring my food. He will leave at night. You can follow him. And be careful — they would kill you.

DAWN.

And in his heart he had been blaming her! For a month, over a month, he had been telling himself over and over, day after day, that he was a fool to think of her as he had been thinking of her; that he was worse than a fool to remember how a wisp of golden-brown hair curved to kiss her cheek; how a sweet, maidenly soul stood tiptoe in her wondrous grey eyes. He had told himself that he was a fool not to see that she was

151

hand in glove with Madden and perhaps Bull Plummer. And now . . .

And now he sat still in the saddle, his face white, his hand gripping the tiny bit of paper which only a great good fortune had brought to him, his hand shaking, a cold fear for her lying in his heart. She had written that just after he had called to her through the closed door, just after she had called to him, "I have nothing to say. Go away!"

More than a month had slipped past, and she had not come back. She had gone away, Madden said. Where? Not to the city, not of her own will. She had gone, with Madden and Plummer threatening her, driving her, to some cave back in the mountains where she could have no opportunity of saying the things they feared to have her say. She had found out the answer to the mystery that Sherrod had found baffling him. She knew their secret.

She knew their secret! A secret which might send both to the penitentiary or perhaps to the gallows. She knew. Was she still alive? A month had passed.

"The Jap, Koto, is to bring my food! He will leave at night!"

"Then, to-night I will know!" muttered Jim Sherrod. "And if they've hurt her, I won't wait to find a lost steer to settle a long account with Bull Plummer. His hands on her throat!"

Riding swiftly, not because there was need for haste but because he could find it possible to wait for night only by doing something, he shot down into the lower valley and sped to the bunkhouse.

"To-night," he told himself, looking impatiently at the high sun, "to-night will bring the beginning of the end. And pray God it finds all well with Dawn Madden!"

CHAPTER
FOURTEEN

For Dawn Madden, these had been days of dread, nights of gloom and terror, a period like a long-drawn-out nightmare that threatened to break that resilient and valiant spirit of hers. At first there had been, despite the despair which so soon began to bear her down, intermittent flashes of hope, because human endurance is based upon hope, because she was young and there had ever been a singing heart within her bosom, because it seemed to her that it was incredible, impossible even, that she could long be held a prisoner here. Every day, every hour at the beginning, she told herself that surely Jim Sherrod would return to the Upper End of his ranch, that he would surely investigate the old log cabin which had already ensnared his interest, that night when Madden had shot at him; that he would find her note. Or if not he, one of his men. That accomplished, she could look in all confidence to Jim Sherrod's coming to her rescue.

But that was only at first. Then she thought that before now the wind would have snatched the folded note from its place and carried it away, perhaps to cover it with leaves, to embed it in a thicket, to bear it fluttering out upon the lake — even to deposit it at

154

Madden's feet, or at Bull Plummer's! And, as hope waned and grew dim and then died, she remembered, too, how from behind a locked door she had called out to Jim Sherrod, "Go away! I have nothing to say to you! *Go away!*" Perhaps he *had* gone away? There was so little telling: she knew nothing, really, of his plans; by now he might be hundreds of miles away, back in the old Painted Rock country.

During all this desolate while she saw never a soul save Madden, the grinning Jap, and Bull Plummer. These three alone knew where she was confined; as a matter of fact Dawn, herself, did not know definitely where she was. As she had said in her brief note to Sherrod, there was a cave, somewhere, high up on the cliffs. She had been bundled out of Madden's house at night, hurried stumbling through the dark, directed into a devious, climbing trail, and finally brought to the cave. Madden led the way; the frog-eyed Jap followed close at her heels; she hastened all that she could lest he lay his hands upon her.

Then followed those interminable days and nights with hope shrinking and finally fading into nothingness, with fear freezing her heart. Most of the time she was alone, but never for an instant did not one of the three hover in the offing, keeping an eye on her when she was outside the cave, watching her, or at the very least the cave entrance, when she withdrew within and flung herself down, helpless and hopeless, on her wretched pile of blankets.

With the passage of these days and nights, both Madden and Bull Plummer, grown surly and always hating each other, came to speak out their thoughts with less and less care whether she overheard or not. To them she was a small, slight thing to be strangled or crushed with a pair of strong hands; they meant that her tongue should not wag, and were fully confident that they could silence her for all time, were that expedient, before she had any chance to tell what she knew and what she more than half suspected. And Bull Plummer, seeing her every day, or every night in the firelight, began to look upon her covetously.

He wanted her, and he meant to have her. She knew the instant that he made up his mind. She saw the new look in his eyes. They lighted up as with an inner fire.

Bull Plummer had had his own troubles that day, though she knew nothing of that. He had done what he did only infrequently; he had drowned his troubles in heavy drinking. He had been more than half drunk when he started up the trail and was still uncertain of speech and gesture when he came to the cliff-top.

The Japanese had come and gone. Madden, surly in his ugly mood, sat on a cracker box just outside the cave door. Somebody had to keep an eye on the girl, night and day, until something was done about the whole matter, and right now the task fell to Madden. He was wishing that he was anywhere else.

Then Bull Plummer came, full of whisky and savagery born of a bad day. He saw Madden, a dark figure in the night against the flickering light of Dawn's fire of dead wood and pine cones. He put his big, hairy hands on his hips and glowered down at the smaller man.

156

"Madden," he said, "I'm getting a bellyful. A bellyful of lots of things lately, of you most of all. You're like a damn tick in a dog's hide. The wonder is I haven't killed you long before now."

"You're drunk, you damned fool," said Madden in his jeering way . . .

"No, I ain't. I'm just sort of half drunk. Just the same, I got a notion to pick you up and drop you down over the cliff edge."

"Try it, Bull," said Madden, and Bull Plummer was sober enough to hear the brittle click of a cocked revolver. He laughed; he clapped Madden on the shoulder.

"I heard your little friend talking, Madden," he said. He squatted down on his heels and clumsily made himself a cigarette. "I want your girl, Madden, and I'm going to have her," he announced as he struck his match.

Madden looked keenly at the heavy face revealed for an instant in the glow of the match. He grunted, uncocked his gun and said in his chill voice:

"Most likely she's listening in on us, Bull."

"What the hell do I care?" said Bull Plummer. Being a man of slight imagination, and one wont to use coined phrases rather than fatigue his brain by seeking words of his own, he said, "I want what I want when I want it. Right now I want Dawn Madden. All for mine. Get me, Madden? And what I want, I get!"

"What do I care what you want?" Madden said in his surly sullen fashion. "And what do I care what you get? The girl?" He shrugged. "Me, I hate the little

157

simple-faced devil, and always did. Ever since her mother —"

Bull Plummer, rocking on his heels, had to laugh again. He even slapped his knee.

"Ever since her mother croaked!" he finished for Madden. "Sure, you've hated the kid; why not? I wouldn't blame you! You married her old lady because she had the hell of a lot of money, and you could use it! Oh, you were a nice looking young gent then, side-whiskers as black as ink and sort of silky, I bet a man! And a white, boiled shirt and a coat with tails, and curly hair and boots all nice and shiny, and a necktie with a phony diamond in it! Oh, my eye and Betty's pet sow!" He kept on rocking in laughter.

"You're drunk, you fool," said Madden the second time.

Bull Plummer got to his feet, towering over the other man, and stood steadily braced, as steady as the rocks about him. He slid his thumbs down into his belt. He said slowly, spacing his words and articulating clearly and distinctly:

"Not quite as drunk as you think, Madden. I know about you, and I'm telling you, and I don't give a single damn if your girl is listening. Of course she is. Ain't you, Dawn?" He grew silent a moment; he cocked an attentive ear toward the cave; when no answer came he spread out his hands in a gesture meaning, "Well, let it go," and picked up the thread of his talk to Madden. He said, "The old lady had the hell of a lot of money, left her by her granddaddy, and so you married her. And, big fool that she was to fall for you, she wasn't fool enough to slip you the dough! Nix. What she did was make a will, leaving the whole wad to Dawn! And so — well, what happened?"

"You idiot! You —"

"Sure. Sure the old lady died! All of a sudden, too! Funny wasn't it? What did you use, Madden? Squirrel poison, rat poison, ground glass?"

Yes, Dawn heard it all, as they knew she did. Bull Plummer in his present mood didn't care. Madden, beginning to figure ahead from this moment, didn't care. Dawn was a negligible piece in the game they were playing. A series of games, rather, it was, with a brand new gambit now.

"You figured," said Bull Plummer, "that all you had to do was keep an eye on the girl for a few years more, until she came of age. Then she'd come into her mama's money. Then you'd grab her by the throat and make her come through. So you kept her on. But she ain't of age yet, Madden, and you're still waiting — and I'm going to have her myself!"

"And the money too, I suppose?" said Madden mildly.

"The money be damned!" roared Bull Plummer. Then he bethought himself and pulled at his lower lip; a broad grin split his face. "Why not?" he wanted to know. "I've got plenty money already for my pork and beans — but who gives a damn if a few more thousands drop in?"

Dawn crouched on the rock floor of her cave, not more than a dozen steps from the two men, shivered and said within herself, "Now I know how girls used to feel on the slave block! Men talking about them as they'd talk about a heifer to be bought and sold! And he did marry my mother just because she had some money — and that is why he has kept me where he thought he wouldn't lose me — until he could get money from me! Oh, thank God he isn't my real father!"

And she thought further, "And so Bull Plummer wants me — just for the money! No, no, it isn't just that. Oh, I wish it was only that! So I could give it to him and go free!" Then, desperate in her fear, she listened to the two men as they went on talking.

"You can have the girl for all of me," said Madden. "As for the money, that's different. I'll split it even with you. Fifty-fifty, Mr. Bull Plummer, or I'll put a spoke in your wheel. Better count about ten before you say no to that proposition. Roll another cigarette, Bull, and think it over."

"I've thought it over for a week!" said Plummer, and choked and swallowed and spat out, "Damn it, man, I want that girl, and I'm going to have her, and if I never get anything else, I'm satisfied!"

Madden jeered at him. "Gone soft, have you, Bull? It's all right with me, but there's just this: If you can get the girl, and the money along with her, you give me a split on the money. Fifty-fifty or I'll cramp your style."

"You and your dirty money! What the hell do I care? I want what I want when I want it — and I get it."

Dawn heard him, his boots scuffling, as he came into the cave — her cave, her only home. She slid her hand under her blankets; she had a gun there, and nobody but Dawn knew that she had it. She thought of Fancy Jim Sherrod shooting a man down — she had called him names — she was ready, God with her, to shoot a man to-night.

Bull Plummer came into her cave. He was trying to play a part, as men do now and then. He said, seeing her through the flickering light:

"You're pretty, Dawn. You're the prettiest thing I ever saw!"

Dawn smiled. Rather, she showed him briefly her small, white teeth. It was a cold smile that she gave Bull Plummer. He should have known. If sober, he would have known. But whisky and Dawn had got into his blood.

"Dawn! You wonderful kid! Me, I'm for you. Dawn, I can get you out of here. I'll even marry you. You'll ride high, wide, and handsome. I'll buy you diamonds. Sure, kid. Me, I love you. You're my girl now."

He opened his arms to her. But she did not come into his embrace. She stepped back, her slim shoulders against the rock wall, her fingers hard on the pistol hidden behind her back.

"Thank you, Mr. Plummer," she said. "But it happens that I'm nobody's girl but my own. And I don't like diamonds. Good-night."

"Your father has promised —"

"Not my father. Just Mr. Madden. He can promise for himself, not for me. Good-night, Mr. Plummer."

He lurched forward. "Dawn, you little fool! Don't be a fool all your life —"

"Not even to-night, Mr. Plummer. You want me, and you want some money that I stand for. Well, neither are for sale right now. And did you hear me tell you good-night? I said it twice!"

"By God, Dawn Madden —"

"Don't swear at me, Bull Plummer. Get out! Leave me alone! If you don't —"

He laughed at her. "If I don't, then what?" he demanded.

"Then I'll shoot you. And I'll shoot to kill!"

Again there was the small, slight metallic click of a gun cocked. This time he heard it. A heavy frown pulled his brows down.

He stood back against the rock wall at the cave's entrance. He built himself, slowly, a cigarette. He licked the edge of the paper, he pulled a slow match up along his thigh, he lighted his smoke. All the while her eyes were on him.

"You're trying to make a whole lot out of nothing, Dawn," he said.

"No. That's not true. I'd rather die —"

"When you're dead, you're dead," said Plummer philosophically. "No sense in that. It's like playing a hand of poker; either you win or you lose. Me, I've got all the high cards. And on top of that, Dawn, I'm crazy about you. I'll be better to you than I ever was to anybody. I'll make you so damn happy, if you'll only travel along with me —"

"Thank you, Mr. Plummer. The answer is no! And now I'd sort of like to be all alone."

"You heard us talking, didn't you?" said Plummer. "Me and your old man. You heard us."

"He's not my old man. He's just Mr. Madden. My mother was very young when she married him. I know. I have her picture. Yes, I heard you. I heard all that I wanted to hear — ever. There are things that you can buy, Mr. Plummer, and there are things that you can't. Things that you can't even have as a free gift — from Mr. Madden. It happens that I belong to me; to myself; I'm not for sale, and I'm not a free gift to —"

"Not to me! But how about Fancy Jim Sherrod? You'd give yourself away if he crooked his little finger!"

She lifted her arching brows at him; she even smiled, like a certain Mona Lisa of long ago.

"Yes?" she said sweetly. "You know so many things, don't you, Mr. Plummer?"

"Don't you know, you fool girl, that I can break you with my two hands?"

"Don't you know, you fool man, that a small lead bullet can send you out of the world? And that my finger is on the trigger?"

CHAPTER
FIFTEEN

"If she is still alive!"

Fancy Jim Sherrod shuddered at the thought of what might have happened during a month of vain search on his part, a month during which the gods of his destiny were good enough to save for him a note hidden where she had placed it. "If she is still kept prisoner here somewhere in the mountains, then the Japanese still carries her her food. And I am going with him."

Fancy Jim Sherrod went about his preparations coolly. It was a crisis in his life of crises, and at such a moment it was his nature and his business to be cool. That was one very good reason why Jim Sherrod had lived to be twenty-nine.

In the late afternoon, but before the boys had come in, he sat in the bunkhouse — he no longer found it necessary to remain aloof in his tent — and carefully cleaned, oiled, and reloaded his guns. Hard Ross, the only man there, watched him with unveiled interest, making no remarks. And Sherrod went on about his business in his silent way.

When he had finished and had put the two heavy revolvers back into their holsters, he made his cigarette with steady fingers, and his eyes went as steadily to meet his foreman's. For a moment the two men regarded each other searchingly.

It was Hard Ross who spoke first.

"The bullet holes in me are feeling pretty good to-day, Jim," he said, with no great expression in his slow tones.

He, too, reached for his tobacco and papers, and again there fell silence in the bunkhouse. Sherrod waited. Ross made and lighted his cigarette, inhaled deeply, leaned back where he sat, and said in the same colourless tone:

"I can ride a horse a short ways, say fifteen or twenty mile, as good's I ever done, Jim. My hand's pretty steady, too."

He lifted his big right hand, the fist clenched, the forefinger pointing, and squinted along it at a knothole in the wall as a man might sight a gun. The forefinger did not waver.

"It's your business, Jim," he said then. "An' I take you to be a man as knows his own business pretty well. But I got my word to say, remember that. I ain't got Silver Slippers back any more than you got your steers. An' — Oh, hell!" he broke off sharply, his voice full of expression now, "let me go along!"

Again there was a silence. The two men smoked, sitting very still, their eyes now and then meeting, now and then turned to a falling ash or to a glimpse of the creek seen through the open door. Slowly Hard Ross's face began to darken, his eyes to grow gloomy. He knew what Sherrod's brief, careful preparations must mean, and he began to fear that when an answer came to him it would be a curt negative. So his stern face brightened visibly when, rising suddenly, Fancy Jim Sherrod put out his hand in a hearty grip.

"I'd rather have you than anybody else, Ross," he said simply. "But are you sure that you are in shape already?"

"I'm real sure," grinned Hard Ross.

He got to his feet, tossed away his newly lighted cigarette, and demanded in his short businesslike tone:

"We're riding real soon?"

"Before the boys come in," Sherrod told him. "Better look to your guns, Ross. We may need them."

"They've been kept in real nice shape," Ross confided to him. And then, "We're riding in the general direction of the Bar Diamond?"

"Not to-night, Ross. But don't let that fool you. I am leaving word for the boys here to be ready for anything that happens. We're going to stir up a little trouble, I think."

When the cook came in to light his fire, Jim Sherrod and Hard Ross went out and down to the corral, leaving a message for the rest of the boys. They roped a couple of the toughest, most spirited horses of the outfit, Hard Ross grinning at the memory of the many times he had roped Sherrod's horse for him, choosing a gentle one. Now as he watched Sherrod's rope swung far out to fall with a dexterity any cowpuncher would have been proud of, Ross grunted:

"A pretty fool I made of myself playing you for a tenderfoot an' picking out a plough horse for you to straddle. Huh!"

166

Sherrod laughed.

"I was devoutly thankful," he returned. "I was afraid that you'd give me a wild one to watch the fun. I'd have had to get myself bucked off, and —"

Hard Ross looked at him, his eyes filled with regret.

"I wish I'd done it! Honest to gran'ma, I wish I'd of done it, Jim! It would almost of made it square with you for making a fool out'n me!"

They saddled, mounted, and rode slowly toward the Upper End, leading a third horse, talking lightly of things which did not matter. And the talk was largely Hard Ross's. He had asked no further questions; he wished to make no reference to the real business in hand until Jim Sherrod reopened the matter. And a sort of boyish glee possessed his spirit at the mere thought of being out on the trail again, at making a move toward Silver Slippers perhaps, at travelling toward a squaring of an old account with the Bar Diamond.

Only when they had ridden to Big Tree Meadow and so out of sight of the bunkhouse and the boys upon the other rim of the valley, did Jim Sherrod tell his foreman what the errand was. At the first mention of Dawn Madden's name, Ross's brows contracted. He had not forgotten the part she had played that night, how her action had abetted Hawley in his coward's attack. To his mind, if she was not of Madden's blood, still she was of Madden's kind; she had taken his name and had shared his interests. And Ross, too, saw in Madden a crook and an accomplice of Bull Plummer.

But long before Sherrod had told his story, Ross's expression changed. It softened in pity as he muttered,

"Pore little girl! She ain't no more'n a kid of a girl anyhow, is she, Jim?" Then it hardened again with wrath, and his big fist clenched at his side.

"It's time Bull Plummer stretched a good piece of tie rope! Put his dirty hands on her throat, huh? Say, Jim," and his voice was suddenly harsh, filled with concern, "you don't reckon — It's been a month! You suppose she's all right, huh?"

Sherrod did not answer. He had been asking himself that question all day while he watched the sun climbing toward the zenith, while he awaited impatiently the lengthening of the afternoon shadows. She was at the mercy of such men as Madden, Bull Plummer, and an ugly dirty Jap! Could all be well with the Dawn Madden?

"We've got to wait for dark, Ross," he said at last. "If they still have her captive and hidden somewhere among these rocks, they must still carry her food to her. That means two things: first, that she is not far from Madden's; and, second, that they will wait for dark."

"We'll hang around an' follow anybody we see leaving the place?" offered Ross quickly.

"Yes. And," Sherrod added sternly, "if we don't see anyone leave, than we'll wait as long as we can; and when we have done that, why, then we'll go in and talk things over with Madden himself!"

In the security of the first hour of darkness they left their horses at the foot of the climb from the valley to the first of the lakes, tying the animals in a dense grove of firs a hundred yards from the trail. Then they went

168

on on foot, walking warily, Sherrod leading, Ross at his heels, eyes and ears alike eager for news of some other person moving about them.

Upon the lake shore they separated.

"You move over that way, Ross," Sherrod whispered. "Keep to the edge of the lake, keep on until you come to the Upper Lake. Hide somewhere near the old cabin and watch."

"An' you, Jim?"

"I'm going to watch over Madden's place. If the damn' Jap goes out to-night, one of us ought to see him."

"If he should get by you?" Ross asked. "If I should see him first, then what? Am I to look you up?"

"You're to waste no time!" answered Sherrod. "You're to follow him and bring Dawn Madden back. That's what I brought you for. But I don't think that I am going to miss him! So long!"

"So long, Jim."

They had spent little time in planning for a night the events of which they made no attempt to forecast. They would find Dawn Madden, if that were possible, and bring her away if they found her. They would go together, following the Japanese, if Fate decided so to dictate; if they were separated, each man would do what he could.

So Jim Sherrod went swiftly, silently, to watch over Madden's place while Hard Ross, crouching down in the shadows at the lakeside, peered through the darkness at the cabin and the small, cleared, rock-floored space about it.

★ ★ ★

It lay in Fate's cold deck that both Fancy Jim Sherrod and Hard Ross were to follow the trail, the dim, hazardous trail that night to the dawn of enlightenment and to Dawn Madden, but that they were not to travel it side by side.

An hour passed. Intolerable stillness hung over the Upper End, broken only at rare intervals by the hoot of an owl, the sharp, snarling bark of a coyote, or the call of a cricket upon the mountain side. There was no wind to make noises in the treetops. The murmur of the water gushing from one lake, through its rocky channel to the other, had long ago blended so harmoniously with the silence as to seem now to be a part of it.

Hard Ross, where he sat, felt his eyeballs grow tired of trying to pierce a black wall which every moment grew blacker, thought longingly upon the cigarette he must forswear, and solaced himself with a generous nibble at his plug cut. Sherrod, his lean body against a giant cedar, watched and waited in growing impatience.

A second hour dragged by. Still there came no sound to tell of a cautious footstep in the darkness, no beam of light to tell of an opened doorway. A third hour went its slow way, and Sherrod tiptoed noiselessly from his hiding-place and sought Ross.

"Seen anything? Heard anything?" he whispered, when at length he had come almost to the cabin door.

"No," grunted Hard Ross. "Hadn't we better go talk with Madden?"

Sherrod hesitated. That was what he wanted to do; that would give them something to do beyond sitting or standing in cramped positions waiting for something which did not happen.

"I'd like to," he admitted softly. "But this is a waiting game, Ross. We might spoil everything. We'll wait another hour."

They did not wait another hour.

Sherrod went back to his tree, Ross dropped down to his place in the shadows. And within fifteen minutes something happened — something that was noticed by Hard Ross, was unseen, unheard by Jim Sherrod. The apelike Japanese had slipped out of the Madden place by some rear exit undreamed of by Sherrod, had moved stealthily through the trees, and had come down to the lake shore.

Ross heard him when the Japanese was not twenty steps from where he crouched, his squatty form dimly outlined when he was not five feet away. And Ross, holding his breath, his every sense on the alert, his own footfall as silent upon the rocky shore as a cat's upon velvet, followed him. A fierce joy leaped up in Hard Ross's heart. At last he was to do his part.

Jim Sherrod, growing more impatient as each moment dragged by, forced himself to wait, telling himself over and over that it was too early to expect anything, that these men would be more than guarded in what they did, that he might have to stay here until midnight. And then, before Hard Ross had followed his quarry ten steps, Jim Sherrod's lax frame grew suddenly tense.

Jim Sherrod in his turn was following his quarry.

He did not at first know who it was that had stealthily opened the front door, having first turned out the lights within, and who now stepped out into the darkness. He could see nothing; he could just hear the soft whine of the door upon its hinges, the soft footfall of a man who went slowly and guardedly. And Sherrod followed.

"It's the damn' Jap!" he told himself with a quick spurt of hope. "He's going to her — and I'm going with him!"

The man who had come out of Madden's house went very slowly at first. He stopped often, and Sherrod knew that he was listening, looking, fearing that he might be seen, heard, followed. So, pausing every few steps, he made his way a hundred yards through the brush clinging about the boles of the great trees.

Then he stopped dead in his tracks, and for five minutes Sherrod could not tell that he had moved. The Up and Down man even began to grow restless, fearing that he had missed the man he thought he was following, dreading that he had slipped away to right or left, noiselessly.

Then the figure, dimly outlined against the surface of the lake, moved on. He was walking swiftly now. In a moment he broke into a run, and Sherrod ran after him keeping fifty steps behind. The man swung about the upper end of the lake; for a moment his hurrying form stood out against a star-silvered strip of the lake; then again it was lost in the thick shadows. There was a moment snatched from pitch darkness into semi-gloom, and the glimpse of a hurrying figure — and Jim

172

Sherrod could not be certain that it was or was not the Japanese. The blurred figure looked a trifle large for the Japanese, but he could not be certain.

The man he followed passed on swiftly now, without a stop, until he came to the cabin against the cliffs upon the far side of the little lake.

"Ross will see him, too!" thought Sherrod. "We'll follow him together!"

He stopped a few paces from the cabin; he heard and half saw that the man before him was at the door, fumbling with the heavy lock, and in the short time allowed him Sherrod moved quietly until he came to the spot where he had left Ross. He put out his hand. He saw what he took to be Ross's big body. He touched it and found that it was a tall stump of a tree. Ross was gone!

"He's near," was Sherrod's quick thought. "He's watching. He'll join me in a minute."

And then he gave his entire attention again to the man at the cabin door. Yet he wondered where Hard Ross was.

Evidently this man sought only to see that the lock had not been tampered with. With a little grunt which Sherrod heard distinctly, he dropped the short chain and turned away, his way leading along the base of the cliffs toward the pass leading into the Bar Diamond valley. And Sherrod, trailing him with a stealth that was like a mountain cat's, with an eagerness which grew keener at each silent step, felt a swift joy leaping up in his heart at the thought that in a little this man would bring him to Dawn.

The trail was one that few men had followed, a trail that Sherrod had never dreamed of. He had to stoop low to slip under a limb of a tree; now and then he had to grope his way through the darkness on hands and knees, feeling his way. He could barely distinguish the form he was following. Suddenly he lost it altogether.

He was close against the base of the cliffs, so close that he had to walk more warily than ever for fear his clothes, brushing against the rough surface, might make just the wee sound that would tell the man ahead that another man trailed him. He felt that the trail was hard rock underfoot; that it clung close to the cliff wall, hidden by the growth of brush and tree; that it began climbing steeply upward. So close was the great, broad, horizontal limb of a big sugar pine growing in the black cañon below that he had come near stepping out upon it instead of the dark path following the ledge of rock, so close that a moment later it may have saved for a little the lives of two men, pursuer and pursued.

For the stealthy step of the man in front had disturbed a stone upon the trail, and it had rolled six inches and lay close to the edge; the quiet step of the man behind touched the same stone and, nicely balanced as it was, it went its noisy way down the cliffside, its racket breaking like thunder against the straining ears of both men.

The figure ahead, not twenty steps ahead, stopped before the stone had grown quiet in the shadows along the ravine bed below. Sherrod stopped as quickly, his nerves taut, his mouth held open a little for his quiet breathing.

174

There followed a period of absolute silence, a stillness as of death or the breathless suspense waiting for death, a stillness which was unbroken for ten minutes during which neither man moved.

And then, again the figure ahead was moving along the trail, so softly that at first Sherrod could not be certain that he heard the almost inaudible footfall upon the hard path. But he was moving — *and he was coming back!* He was going to make doubly sure that he was not followed.

In the daytime two men could not have met and passed here; there was scant room for one. Jim Sherrod's mind desperately seeking a way out, a way to avoid discovery, at first saw no way. He could not move back, too, for he knew that his foot might strike another stone, that he might be discovered. He could tell that the footsteps were coming toward him more swiftly now, with less and less caution.

If he were discovered, what would be the end? It would mean that he had lost his chance to follow this man to Dawn Madden; it would mean perhaps a struggle on the narrow trail and an end of things for them both. Both men, locked in a death grip, might go plunging down into the rock-bed of the gorge below, and neither ever even know who the other was.

And then, thinking swiftly, he hit upon the one chance and took it. The broad limb of the tree at his side invited him. He stepped out boldly, bending down, stooping low, clutching it with hands and knees, balanced a moment, and then with no sound but the rustling of leaves which was lost in the faint rush of

175

water below, he sat on the limb of the big pine, not two feet from the narrow trail.

And just in time! He could see the returning figure now, could hear the low breathing, and as the man came abreast of him, only a couple of feet away, he could at last make out who it was. It was not the Jap.

It was Madden himself.

Madden paused again and stood leaning forward, peering into the darkness swallowing up the downward trail. Sherrod could have shot out a quick hand and plucked him from where he stood. Only for an instant did Madden hesitate here; then, hurrying now, making all the speed that he dared make upon so hazardous a way, he was hastening downward, back along the way he had come. Sherrod heard his footsteps echo loudly until they died out, and he knew that Madden had gone nearly back to the cabin.

"He's making sure," Sherrod told himself again. "He isn't taking any chances that aren't in the game. And he'll come back this way when he's convinced."

So he sat upon his limb, balancing, holding to the branches about him, drawing a little farther back from the trail and waited. And in ten minutes Madden came back. He was walking swiftly now. He was making what haste he could and throwing caution to the winds, evidently in a very great hurry, evidently assured that it had been no human foot behind him to set the stone rolling.

"My luck's with me," muttered Sherrod as once more he set foot upon the trail, reaching out easily from his tree. "I know who I'm following now, and it's going to be easier to trail him now that he's making most of the noise."

He jerked off his boots, carrying them in one hand, and hurried on, unmindful of bruises and cuts from the flinty, sharp fragments of granite strewing the trail. He could hurry now, even as Madden was hurrying, and with no grating of leathern sole on rock to whisper of his coming.

For fifteen minutes the way led straight toward the top of the Bar Diamond pass, climbing steeply. Then there was a little wider shelf, a sort of natural platform, and pausing here a moment Sherrod could hear Madden's footfall almost directly above him. For here the trail turned and wound backward along the cliffs, still climbing but leading in an opposite direction, away from the pass.

For another fifteen minutes Sherrod followed, and during that time, and two or three times, he saw Madden's form outlined against the sky above him. They were coming close to the top of the cliffs.

It was hard climbing now. The trail was scarcely more a trail than was that steep climb up to the crest of Daybreak Spire. Sherrod gripped at the face of the rock with his two hands, fastening his boot straps to his belt to have all his fingers free, pulled himself up where he had seen the blurred form of Madden go, held his body tightpressed against the steep walls of granite, trying not to think of the sheer fall below him.

But where Madden had gone he could go, and he made his grim way uncomplainingly. If he should only find Dawn at the end of the trail, if all were still well with her, no trail would be too difficult.

At last Madden had come to the top of the cliffs. For just an instant his silhouette was sharply defined against the clear sky; then it was lost again as suddenly as it had materialized from the shadows. So quickly was it gone that, for a moment, Sherrod feared the man had fallen down into some gorge upon the other side of the cliff wall.

Then Sherrod came on swiftly, fearing that if Madden had not fallen, at least he was lost to him among the boulders he expected to find strewing the ridge. But though he climbed with what speed he could, he moved with what caution was possible.

He drew himself up by his hands; he threw himself flat on his stomach and wriggled up to the spot where he had last seen Madden. He lifted his head a little and dropped back, lying flat against the rocks.

The leaping flames of a brush fire had startled him, the fire looked so close, the cliffs about were so bright with the quivering, rosy light. He had seen Madden again in that swift glimpse, had seen that the man he had followed stood upon a boulder upon the south slope of the cliffs, had seen the Japanese, had seen Hard Ross, had seen Dawn Madden. And, background for the picture so vividly limned before his startled eyes, was the wildest bit of the mountains he had ever seen, rugged, high-lifted spires and pinnacles of rock, fathomless, sheer-walled gorges filled with inky darkness.

178

Madden stood upon a hog's-back, a spine of rock cresting the cliffs and of almost knife sharpness and thinness with a straight drop to the north into the valley of the Twin Lakes, a straight drop to the south into a cañon a thousand feet deep. Here at the top it was a mere distance of twenty feet across the gorge.

It was across the gorge upon a flat surface perhaps a dozen feet square that the fire was burning. The leaping flames showed the yawning mouth of a cave just beyond the level space, and Dawn Madden standing there. It showed a bridge running across the chasm, a bridge of one piece of timber rough-hewn from a log, not over six inches thick, some two feet wide. One end of the narrow bridge rested upon the broad rock in front of the cave, the other end lay upon a flat-topped boulder upon Madden's side of the chasm.

Walking swiftly across the timber which trembled under his fearless stride was the apelike Jap, carrying a parcel in his hands. Because the Japanese was forced to give all of his attention to the placing of one foot before the other, and because he could not look behind him, Hard Ross was no longer seeking to conceal himself. He stood watching, stood at the brink of the chasm only a few feet from the Japanese — *only a few feet from where Madden was watching* him!

Sherrod saw that Hard Ross had his gun in his hand now, that he was ready — ready for what? For whatever lay before him, but all unconscious of what was behind him! And Sherrod saw that Madden, too, had a revolver in his hand, and that he was watching Hard Ross.

179

And Dawn Madden, seeing them all in the firelight, cried out in alarm and in warning. She saw Jim Sherrod as he rose swiftly a dozen paces behind Madden and threw up his hand — and she clapped her hand to her mouth. He could see the look of terror in her widening eyes. He could see Hard Ross move out a little and knew that he was going to call to the Japanese to throw up his hands. He could see Madden jerk up his right hand and knew that he was not going to call out, that he was going to shoot without warning.

And then, suddenly Jim Sherrod sprang forward and downward, his hands going to Madden's throat, jerking him back to the ground.

"Cover the Jap, Ross!" shouted Sherrod. "Shoot him if he tries anything! I've got Madden. Don't take any chances now!"

"I've got him covered," Hard Ross's voice floated back to him coolly. "With two guns, Jim. I ain't taking no chances. But — but I'm sort of glad you come along, Jim!"

180

CHAPTER
SIXTEEN

Madden's sharp cry, choked out of him, rang wildly, a bullet from his revolver winged its way over the top of the cliff on the far side of the gorge, and Madden learned what strength might lie in a pair of white hands as he was flung backward upon the ground, his gun jerked from his hand.

The Japanese, already more than halfway across the shaking bridge, leaped forward as he guessed exactly what had happened behind him. Sherrod saw the parcel fall from the Oriental's hand, saw it drop into the nothingness which yawned hungrily below, and heard Hard Ross's voice booming out loudly in a short:

"Up with your hands, you Jappy! Quick, or I'll let starlight through you!"

"We've got the drop on them!" was Sherrod's quick thought.

Then he heard Dawn Madden's voice in a terrified scream, saw her spring backward through the mouth of the cave, saw her snatch up a heavy blanket from the ground, and before he could guess her thought she had flung it over the leaping flames of her brush fire. Another blanket followed and another. This he could not see, for the first one had killed the light which had befriended him and Hard Ross. It was dark, pitch dark again. He could not see the form struggling in his hands, he could not see Ross or the Jap or Dawn.

"Hell!" shouted Hard Ross. "Damn it, girl, are you crazy?"

In a flash the advantage had switched. The Oriental was at the girl's side. The narrow bridge lay between them and Ross and Sherrod. Madden was giving Sherrod all the trouble he wanted. A raging anger leaped high in Sherrod's heart.

"She has double-crossed us, Ross!" he shouted. "Look out! God knows what we're up against!"

"An' the devil cares!" Ross yelled back at him lustily. "Can you manage Madden all right?"

"Yes. But —"

"Then I'll watch this little bridge here. I reckon they can't get out no other way. An' the first one as comes acrost is going to get dropped about a million feet into nowhere."

There had come no word from Dawn. But it came now, in a strangling scream:

"I had to put out the fire! Bull Plummer's here! He — Oh, God!"

The scream died in her throat. There came a spurt of flame, and a bullet fired from a ledge of rock just above the entrance to the cave sang its way through the night over Sherrod's head. But he had understood; he knew the meaning of the strangling cry; he knew that either the yellow hands of the slinking Jap or Plummer's hands or the hands of one of Plummer's men were on her throat, that only her quick action in throwing the

182

blanket on the fire had saved him, and the command he muttered into Madden's ear was full of menace.

Sherrod dropped to the ground, holding Madden's struggling body close to him. He had Madden's two wrists in his iron grip. He bent them back until they came together behind Madden's back.

And then, as silently as he could, he dragged Madden with him toward the spot where a moment ago he had seen Hard Ross.

"You cry out," he hissed into Madden's ear, "and there's nothing left for me but to kill you! Be still!"

After a moment of blind groping he came to Ross's side.

"Help me, Ross," he whispered. "We've got to tie him and jam something down his throat so he can't yell. Hurry!"

Two belts and a couple of neck-scarfs did the business. Madden lay still now, his mouth pried wide open with a bit of silk trailing forth. Jim Sherrod and Hard Ross standing side by side, close to the end of the rough-hewn plank, stared across the gulf of darkness into deeper darkness, and tried to guess what was happening a bare twenty feet from them.

"Plummer an' the Jap have got her," whispered Ross. "There ain't much chance on their troubling us over her, but —"

"But," whispered Sherrod, "what is going to happen to her? Are we going to wait here until daylight to find out? There's bound to be some other way out of this place. They'll be gone by morning!"

He broke off sharply. He did not like to think what might happen to the girl long before morning came. She had been hidden here for a month. Why? Because she knew something which Madden and Plummer did not want her to tell. Now, to-night, it had been her action which had saved Sherrod and Ross from Plummer's fire and Plummer's anger.

That note which he had found in the chinks of the old cabin wall had been a cry to him for help. He had come, he was almost at her side, and now she needed him if she ever needed him. Was he going to wait here, a bare twenty feet away from her, and let happen what might?

"I'm going over there!" Sherrod whispered into Hard Ross's ear. "It's taking chances, yes. But, God, man! What chances is she taking?"

And he gripped Hard Ross's hand hard, hard, when the whispered answer came back to him:

"I'm glad it's dark, Jim. I always get dizzy when I can see down so far under me!"

Not another sound had come across to them from the far side of the chasm. But they knew that somewhere there Plummer and the Japanese waited and watched. They knew that Dawn Madden's lips had been silenced, perhaps she had been only gagged — that they could not know.

"I'm going across now, Ross," Sherrod again was whispering. "I don't think that they'll expect it — so soon."

"I'm behind you," returned Ross quietly. "It's a fool thing, but I guess it's the only way. An', Jim —"

184

"Yes?"

"If they jump you as you land, throw yourself to the left. I'll shoot to the right. *Sabe?*"

Then they moved forward. Jim Sherrod, going first, crept on his hands and knees until his groping fingers found the end of the plank. And then a quick thought came to him and he stopped.

He knew what one of the men would be doing upon the other side of the gorge, knew so well that the realization was a flash of inspiration. It was as if he could see the man. Plummer or Madden's Jap was standing at Dawn's side, holding her, a rude hand over her mouth perhaps. And the other man? He would be lying stretched out on the ground at the other end of the plank. His fingers resting upon it would tell him the instant that a man set foot upon it. Sherrod had seen already how the slight bridge trembled and shook under a crossing foot.

"Plummer will be the one lying there," thought Sherrod swiftly. "He'd know the second I was crossing. He'd wait until I was halfway and then a quick shove to the end of the board and I'd drop a thousand feet! I'd be walking to my death with my eyes open, like a fool!"

He drew back, hesitating. He could not help Dawn Madden that way, and yet he must help her some way. Had she not suffered enough, alone unaided, during the past month?

"What's the matter, Jim?" whispered Hard Ross. "Can't you find the plank?"

"Yes. Come here."

He drew Ross backward with him until the two men stood at a safer distance from any ears to overhear them, and then told Ross his thought briefly.

Ross swore under his breath.

"That's their game!" he whispered savagely. "The lowdown curs. And now what? It's wait until —"

It had been dead still upon the other side of the gorge. Now, without warning a revolver barked and spat, a red spurt of flame split the darkness only to be swallowed up by the darkness again, and the whine of a bullet told them that Plummer and the Japanese were watching, listening.

"An' we can't shoot back!" groaned Ross as he glared back, his gun frozen tight in the grip of his hand. "We might hit her!"

"Meanwhile there's not a chance in a thousand of them hitting us," Sherrod answered coolly. "Here's a puzzle, Ross. What's the answer?"

"I'd give ten dollars for a cigarette," groaned Ross. And then he groaned, "There ain't no answer."

But there must be! Jim Sherrod considered only that she had called to him; that he had come so near; that he must find a way.

"If she hadn't put the fire out!" Ross was muttering.

"If she hadn't, Plummer would have put a bullet hole in both of us," cut in Sherrod shortly. "For a second it was a mighty good thing for us that it was dark. Now if we had the light again; — by the Lord, Ross, we've got to build another fire!"

"An' get picked off while we're scratchin' a match?" grunted Ross. "I don't like it."

But Sherrod had his inspiration, and he was acting on it without a moment's delay. He began groping along the cliffs for dry brush, bits of wood and grass, anything that would burn. Ross, understanding that Sherrod had made up his mind, followed suit.

It was slow work, what with the blackness of the night and the scarcity of any growth here upon the heights. But in fifteen minutes they had collected a goodly pile of combustible stuff, and at Sherrod's low-spoken command Hard Ross helped him pile it.

Now, while seeking the material for his fire, Sherrod had shaped his plan definitely, studying the ground as he went. Ten feet to the right of the near end of the plank was a big boulder standing close to the edge of the precipice. Moving silently, crouching low, he and Ross made the pile of brushwood just to the right of the boulder, just at the brink of the chasm. Then Hard Ross, grasping the plan, moved as Sherrod directed until he had gone another ten feet from the end of the plank, where he crouched down in a little hollow deep enough to partly conceal his body.

Sherrod slipped behind the boulder, and with his body hidden from Plummer and the Japanese, struck his match. A little dry grass served as a lighter. The flame broke out. brightly, and he tossed the burning wisp to his bonfire, slipping back swiftly behind his rock.

There came a snarl from across the narrow ravine; he knew that it was Bull Plummer's voice, and that Plummer understood; and then two revolvers, Plummer's and the Jap, Koto's, cracked their warning as two bullets whizzed by the rock behind which Sherrod had withdrawn.

In a moment other dry grass caught fire, the twigs of the dead brush sucked at the twisting flames, and the firelight ran up as if it were following a powder train. A gleam of light cleft the darkness and showed the mouth of the cave. Dawn was not there. She had been thrust back through the entrance to be out of the way.

Plummer stood for a moment in sight, the Japanese at his side. But before Hard Ross could fire, both men had leaped a little to the side, and the darkness befriended them again.

Now was the time Jim Sherrod had set for his action, an action full of danger but not impossible of success if he did not loiter. The big boulder against which his fire was growing every second stood just between the leaping flames and the end of the plank; the end of the plank was still in pitch darkness.

He slipped around the boulder. Hard Ross, playing his part, opened fire at the spot where Plummer and the Nipponese had disappeared and succeeded in drawing their fire. And then Jim Sherrod, taking his chance, set his foot upon the most perilous bridge a man ever sought to travel.

He crouched low; he found the rough surface of the plank with his hands; he half straightened, waited one second until he could see before him, wavering and unreal, the way across the chasm, heard Ross's fire and the shots from the other side, steadied himself, and started.

Ross was shooting with both hands and certainly making enough racket for two men with two guns. There was no reason why Plummer and the Japanese should suspect that Sherrod was crossing. He must travel that dangerous way slowly. He must edge onward, mincing step after mincing step as he balanced over the open jaws of death below. He must come halfway, over halfway until he was at the edge of the spreading circle of light, and then in one leap reach the far side.

"Good old Ross!" he muttered. "God bless him!"

For Ross was still firing like two men, and he was talking now, muttering things to Jim as if Jim were at his side, saying:

"A little more to the right, Jim! Keep down, Jim! Hurt bad, Jim!"

And Jim Sherrod was already very nearly halfway across the trembling bridge!

Almost halfway! A little more and he could straighten up, take a swift step into the light, and spring to the far side. He would take his chances then, but in the uncertain light with Plummer and the damn Jap driven a little farther by Ross's fire, with the sudden dart he would make, throwing his body sidewise, into the darkness upon the other side of the cave, he thought that the chances were with him. Another three or four cautious steps and . . .

There came a shout, a shrill yell of warning — Madden's voice. Madden had somehow gotten the gag out of his mouth.

"Look out!" he shrieked. "Sherrod's on the bridge!"

And then Sherrod did not know rightly what happened. He ran now; he must run or a bullet would drop him. He did not know how far he had to go, but the far brink did not look eight feet away, and a bullet whizzed over his head and he jumped for it — leaped far out, throwing his arms forward, to fall sprawling, to feel his ankles strike upon the edge, to know that his body had landed safely.

He drew himself up. He twisted to the side. He half-rolled, half-crawled, straightened, and plunged into the shadows. There had come another bullet near him, and he did not hear its whining song. For this bullet had not missed, and he felt his left arm go nerveless and limp.

Madden had shouted again and again.

Then Sherrod heard running feet, guessed wildly that Madden had freed himself from his rude handcuffs and was rushing upon Hard Ross. He heard Ross cry out. He thought that at last one of the bullets from the other side of the cave had struck the big foreman, and then he knew that Madden and Ross were struggling, swaying upon the brink of the chasm.

"My God!" cried Sherrod, forgetting his own wound. "He's hurt and Madden has struck him from behind. Ross! Ross!"

But Hard Ross did not answer. Dimly Sherrod descried the two forms swaying insecurely upon the edge of the cliffs. He dared not shoot; he could not tell which was Madden, which was Ross.

Then again he heard a man cry out in a strangling, terrified scream. He could not tell whether the voice was Ross's or Madden's. And then — then there was only one man on the far side, drawing himself away weakly from the death which had caught the other man's slipping feet. Was it Madden? Was it Hard Ross?

But there was not time for a question now, not even the question of the death of friend or enemy. Sherrod heard the wild scream echoing through the cliffs, heard a body strike and fall and strike again, and already he was braced against a rock, his left arm useless at his side, his right hand gripping his gun and firing at the blurred forms of Plummer and the Japanese. And he was firing slowly, carefully, with no thought of wasting lead.

The two blurred forms disappeared; he could not tell whether his bullets had found their targets or not. He waited and listened. He heard quick steps, the rolling of a stone; he thought that they were drawing back. And then he called sharply half afraid of the silence which might answer him —

"Ross!"

And Hard Ross's big voice boomed back —

"All right, Jim!"

Jim Sherrod drew deep the breath of gratitude into his lungs. Ross was all right, Dawn was all right. Sherrod counted himself as good as new. And there was left nothing to be done but a little clean fighting, with no odds.

He felt of his wounded arm with firm fingers. No bone was broken; there was only a severe but not dangerous wound through the bulge of the forearm. He picked up the gun which he had dropped, jammed it into his holster, gripped the other weapon in his right hand, and turned his eyes toward the cave.

And then he saw Dawn Madden coming swiftly toward him, saw her face deathly white in the firelight.

"Was it — Mr. Madden who — fell?" she asked faintly.

"Yes!" Sherrod cried. "But step back. They haven't gone yet and —"

She came on, walking steadily, still swiftly, standing out unhidden in the firelight.

"They have gone," she answered quietly. "I know."

She came on until she was close to Jim Sherrod's side.

"You have been good to me," she said faintly. "You have come to me when I needed you most. And — and I am sorry —"

Now her voice came to him faintly, hardly more than a shaken whisper.

"Sorry?" he asked, wondering. "That I came?"

"No, no," she told him quickly, seeking to steady her voice. "If you had not come —" She broke off with a shudder. "What might have happened! It is too hideous to think about!"

"Then you must not be sorry for anything," he said gently.

"But I must tell you, I must try to tell you, that I am sorry and ashamed — that I said I would rather be dead than touch you!"

And suddenly she reached out and lifting her two hands laid them upon his shoulders.

"I never understood!" she told him swiftly. "How could I know such things? That there were men living whom another man must not think of mercifully? That there were men like Plummer — and Mr. Madden! You have been good to me, Jim Sherrod," she whispered.

His hands crept upward, closing about hers on his shoulders, drawing them down. He was not even conscious of the pain in his wounded arm.

"You poor little Dawn Maiden," he said softly in a voice grown husky.

"Take me away with you!" she cried passionately, with a frightened glance into the darkness about them. "I think I have nearly gone mad! I would go mad! You will take me away with you, won't you, Jim Sherrod? Oh, I know that they have gone. And I am lost and frightened! And I'll tell you all about it. I have so much to tell you."

Then because she seemed suddenly so little a Dawn Maiden, and because she was trembling, seemingly about to fall, and because he could not help it, he caught her in his arms and held her close. Once before had he held her like this, and she had flung herself shuddering out of his arms. But now she clung very tight to him.

Hard Ross was coming across the narrow foot-bridge and grinning broadly as he came.

CHAPTER
SEVENTEEN

There were two trails leading down, Dawn said. One went its steep way to the Bar Diamond, the other Sherrod and Ross had followed here to-night from the lake.

"We must hurry," she insisted. "Don't make me talk now, will you? I have so much to tell you, but you will let it go until we get —"

She broke off and turned away. Sherrod fancied that the word "home" was trembling on her lips. Home! What home was hers now?

"Until we get down into the valley," she went on bravely. "To your bunkhouse."

She slipped out of Sherrod's arms and stood leaning against the rocks, staring outward and downward. He saw that her eyes had been drawn involuntarily toward the abyss down into which Madden had plunged head-long; he knew that her thoughts had followed the wild plunge downward, and the convulsive shudder which he saw ripple through her tired body hurt him. But she had not once mentioned Madden's name after being assured that he it was who had fallen; she would never mention his name again after she had done with telling her story.

"Before we leave," she directed in a moment, "I want you to go in there and see the place in which I have stayed for a month. There is a lantern. I will wait here."

Sherrod went swiftly to the cave, found the lantern at the side of the wide entrance, and lighted it. Hard Ross had come to his side.

"Hurt bad, Jim?" he whispered.

"No," Sherrod returned hurriedly. "And there's no reason why she should know anything about it."

Ross nodded. The two men turned their eyes into the cave as the weak rays from the lantern brought out the scant details. It was a rock-walled chamber some twenty feet deep, half that wide. It was perhaps six feet high at the front, not over three feet high at the rear. There was no sign of a chair or table; the only bed had consisted of the three blankets which Dawn had thrown upon the fire; there was no rug, no book, no single thing to give a little touch of comfort. Sherrod frowned as he looked, Ross cursed softly.

"An' they made her stay here a month! Pore little lady! What is it they were afraid of her telling, Jim? About the cattle, huh?"

"We'll know soon, Ross." Sherrod turned out the lantern and came hurriedly out of the cave. "It must have been a month of hell for a girl like her, Ross!"

Ross's hand was on his shoulder, Ross was whispering urgently:

"As soon's she begins to talk, Jim, you'll ask her if she knows anything about Silver Slippers, won't you?"

"You saw?" Dawn asked gently. "It's nearly driven me crazy. I think they wanted me to go mad — or to

195

die! I was alone; I was half starved. They gave me food and water only at night, and then not enough of either. But now, we must hurry before it is too late!"

"Too late?" repeated Sherrod.

"Yes! Come. I will tell you everything when we get down."

So they made their way back across the narrow bridge, Dawn Madden's hand held tight in Sherrod's as she walked behind him, Hard Ross coming across last.

"Draw the plank over this side," Dawn said then. "They can't follow us this way if you do."

Ross drew in the plank, and they began their way down. Dawn's strength was not what it had been that other night when she had hurried on down Daybreak Spire ahead of Sherrod, but she did not once complain and often led the way to show them the trail, which she knew better than they. And yet it was an hour before they made their way down to the floor of the valley at the side of the lake.

"Do you want to stop here and rest?" Sherrod asked.

"No, no!" she cried quickly. "There is no time; we must hurry on. I am afraid —"

"Of what?" asked Sherrod wondering.

"I'll tell you when I tell everything," she answered a little stubbornly. "And now, won't you hurry? Please?"

Then they found the horses where earlier in the night they had tethered them, Sherrod used one hand to help Dawn to the back of the animal they had brought for her, and they rode swiftly to the bunkhouse. It was with the first firm streaks of the morning in the sky behind them that they came into the home corrals.

196

Only a word did Dawn say then.

"While you unsaddle," she said to Sherrod as she slipped to the ground, "let Ross hurry on and wake the rest. I think you'll want all of your men to hear what I have to say."

Getting a quick nod from his employer, Ross hurried away on his errand. Sherrod left the horses, still saddled, in the corral, closed the gate, and he and Dawn walked slowly to the bunkhouse.

It doesn't take a cowpuncher long to get out of bed and get his clothes on when there is the slightest need of haste. Before half of Hard Ross's brief order had been given, blankets had been thrown off, bare feet had struck the floor, men were asking swift questions as their hands ran out for the garments scattered untidily upon chairs and floor. And when Dawn Madden and Jim Sherrod came to the bunkhouse, the door was wide open, the lamps were lighted, and the whole force of the Up and Down, tousled and unkempt, was ready to greet them.

The cook needed no prodding. He took one look at the girl's face, his shrewd eyes travelled to the boss's set mouth and hard eyes, and he built his fire and put on coffee and bacon with hastening hands.

A dozen hands were ready to make the girl comfortable. The best chair in the house was dragged forward, dusted and examined for a treacherous broken leg, odds and ends of clothing and general range riff-raff were thrust hastily out of sight under bunks. Men sought and donned coats to mark their respect, and had equally little care as to ownership and fit of the garment into whose sleeves they thrust their arms. And Dawn Madden, smiling at them a little wanly, thanking them softly, dropped wearily into her chair and wearily began her story.

"It has been going on a long, long time," she said. "For years, I think. I don't know how long. And, though I suspected Plummer, I never dreamed of the whole truth until that night when I built the fire which nearly cost Ross his life.

"Mr. Madden" — they all noted that whenever she was forced to mention him she called him Mr. Madden — "had me build the fire. I know now that Plummer told him to do it. Plummer was at the house late that afternoon. I heard them mention Hawley, Silver Slippers, Ross. I did not think much of it at the time. I know now that Mr. Madden had me do it because he was afraid to do it himself, afraid that someone would shoot him. I don't know whether he was afraid of Ross or of Plummer."

"Of Plummer?" asked Sherrod curiously.

"Yes. He and Plummer have been side by side all this long while, and yet I think that they distrusted each other. I know that more than once they have quarrelled. I think that they hated each other. It required a great, mutual danger to make them sure of each other.

"Anyway, I made the fire. I saw Hawley's attack upon Ross, I saw Mr. Sherrod shoot Hawley, I heard Mr. Madden refuse to allow a wounded man to be brought into his house. I should have told everything then, but I knew nothing. I had only my suspicions. I was terribly nervous, and I wanted time to think. Then, in the early morning, when I came back I came unexpectedly upon Plummer and Mr. Madden, I overheard what they were saying, and I knew that during that same terrible night they had driven off fifty head of Up and Down cattle. I *knew* then what I had suspected; I knew that they were cattle thieves! And I learned what they had done with the stolen stock!"

Every man there leaned a little closer to her at those words, every eye brightened perceptibly. There was a long score to settle, and this began to look like the time for settlement.

"I tried to slip away without them hearing me," Dawn went on. "I wanted to run back to Mr. Sherrod and to tell him. But they heard me; Plummer caught me and dragged me back; Mr. Madden threatened me. Then I heard Mr. Sherrod asking for me. I heard what Mr. Madden told him. I heard him come to the door of the room in which Plummer was watching over me.

"Plummer had his big hand on my throat. He whispered to me that if I did not send you away he would throw open the door and shoot you down — that he would kill Ross — that I would be forcing him to it. And, because there was nothing left to do, I sent you away!

"I knew then, with their secret in my hands, they would not again let me have an opportunity to get word to you. I feared that they would do just the thing which they did do. So, in the little time I had while Plummer and Mr. Madden were in the hallway, talking in low

199

whispers, I ran to my desk and wrote the note which Mr. Sherrod found last night."

"You slipped it between the logs of the old cabin as you went by?" asked Sherrod.

"Yes. I knew that Mr. Madden never went near the old cabin in the daytime, and I felt that there would be little danger of his seeing it there. I hoped that you or one of the men would find it. It was the only thing I could do. And now for the secret I learned! I must tell it quickly; if you can reach the place before they do you will find your cattle there — every head. Oh, it was so simple a thing for them to do!"

She paused a moment, her face looking very white and tired. And then, her big grey eyes upon Jim Sherrod, she ran on quickly:

"I could have told you up at the Upper End to-night, but I was afraid for you and Ross! We came right by the place; I knew that if I told you, nothing would hold you back, and that you would rush into danger, just you two alone. I was afraid that you might find Plummer already there, and his men with him. I wanted you to come here first, to get all of your men to go with you. I am afraid that things have come to a desperate point. When you know all that I have to tell you, it will be as if there were a rope around Bull Plummer's neck, a rope around the neck of nearly every one of the men taking his pay. And they are not the kind of men to give in without a fight."

Then she told them the last word of her story. The men looked down from her to one another, their eyes widening.

"Good Lord!" muttered Hard Ross. "We'd ought to of guessed it a year ago!"

Ten minutes later Fancy Jim Sherrod with nine men at his back, was riding again the trail to the Upper End. Every man was armed, every man stern-eyed and ready for what might lie hidden in the new breaking day.

"An' me," Hard Ross grunted to himself with vast satisfaction, "I'm going to ride home on Silver Slippers, the old-son-of-a-gun!"

CHAPTER
EIGHTEEN

The sun was up, the twin lakes glistened with the fulfilled promise of the new day. The ten cowboys, riding swiftly, had come to the Upper End. Fancy Jim Sherrod, still a horse's length in the lead, drew rein just before he came to the spot where the old cabin stood close to the lake shore. As if at a spoken command his men stopped with him.

"Boys," said Sherrod slowly, a little sternly, "I don't know what I'm leading you into this morning. I don't know whose saddle may go home empty. If any man of you dislikes the job, if any man of you doesn't want to take upon himself a part of another man's work, now is a good time to go back!"

He waited a moment. The cowboys who had followed him returned his steady gaze steadily. They had heard; they did not speak an answer in words, but their eyes spoke for them. Sherrod turned a little in his saddle, looking from the first to the last of them.

"Thank you, boys," he said quietly. "I knew it. But listen a little, first. This is my game! I am playing it my way. And," his voice ringing sharp, grown more stern then before, "if any man of you is going to try to take it upon himself to say what shall be done, I don't want him. He can go back now! I say I am playing this my way. You are to do what I say or go back."

Still they made no answer, still their eyes held steadily to his. A month ago no man of them would have taken an order from Jim Sherrod at a time like this. This morning they were very content to let him play his game his way.

"All right," he called curtly to them. "Now, stay where you are and keep your eyes open until I ask for you. Ross, Harper, Happy, you come ahead with the crowbar and axes."

As their names were called, they shot their spurs home, and their eager horses leaped to Sherrod's side. He, too, had ridden on, dismounting at the door of the old log cabin.

"Make short work of it, boys," he commanded. "Try the door first. It's lined on the inside with sheet-iron, but I think we can smash the door off its hinges."

Then they fell to their work with a will. The hush of the valley died among clanging echoes as bar and axe struck through the rotting planks and rang against the iron wall. In a few minutes they had torn the heavy padlocks from their chains, twisted and broken the thick staples, wrecked the hinges, and the way was open.

The door fell noisily.

"Now!" Sherrod was leading his horse through the narrow opening. "Come ahead. But no matter what we run up against, don't start anything until I say so!"

His first glance into the cabin told him that Dawn Madden had made no mistake. The floor underneath was like the ground out in front, hard rock strewn with flinty fragments of granite. The walls, three of them were of sheet iron. The fourth, the wall against the cliffs — there was no wall there! There was just a yawning hole into the rock through which three big steers might have passed abreast; there was just a sort of tunnel running back some fifty yards, and then . . .

Sherrod was again in the saddle; he had ridden through, and an exclamation of amazement broke from his lips. He was upon the rim of a tiny valley, a valley lying between the Up and Down and the Bar Diamond, measuring some hundred yards across at the widest spot, being some five or six hundred yards long.

The cliffs rose straight about it on all sides, bare, barren, so steep that it was almost an impossibility for a man to climb them anywhere. There was nothing but rock and scant, drying, torn brush here; there was no grazing land for cattle. But there was straw; there were long troughs where stock could be watered; there was every sign that a large herd had fed here very recently.

"No wonder we never found this place," grunted Hard Ross. "Look up there, Jim! A man could never climb up anywhere from the outside so's he could look down on it."

"An' old Madden doing the foxy stunt of building that old cabin slam up against the hole in the cliffs!" supplemented Sunny Harper. "That made it as safe as a church! Think of him doing that more'n twenty years ago, an' working his little old game off an' on all that time! The darned old pie-rat!"

"Anyway," said Hard Ross as his quick eyes sought and did not find Silver Slippers, "Plummer's been here ahead of us an' has hazed the stock on out. There must be another way out."

"Through the old rock an' log corrals at the upper end of the Bar Diamond!" cried Happy Day. "He's crowded 'em out through there!"

"Come on!" called Sherrod. "They haven't much the head start of us. But keep your eyes open. Plummer will know we're trailing him by this time. They'll be looking for us."

They rode hastily through the tiny, hidden valley, sweeping onward through the shadows flung downward by the cliffs a thousand feet above. And though their horses were racing now, they had gone only a half of the way to the narrow exit five hundred yards away when they were given leaden assurance that Plummer was looking for them.

A rifle broke the stillness with its snapping bark, the echoes rolled like thunder among the cliffs, and the horse ridden by Mute Adams, reared, screamed, and came down with a broken leg. Mute swore, disentangled himself from his stirrups, and rolled himself out of the way. Before he had ceased rolling or swearing, both Sunny Harper and Happy Day had thrown their rifles to their shoulders and had fired back at the shaking shrub and little puff of smoke hanging over the mouth of the exit. Then there was sudden, deep silence.

"Just a sharpshooter, more to signal to Plummer than anything else," decided Sherrod. "Sunny, you and Happy ride up in front with me, just the same. Take a shot at anything you see moving."

Again they swept on, Mute Adams running after them on foot, crying angrily for them not to leave him out of it, for one of them to take him up behind the saddle. Little John thoughtfully reined in a moment, Mute climbed up and the two of them riding a horse unused to carrying double, and trying at every jump to get its head down and buck them off, clattered along noisily in the wake of the race.

Where the way narrowed to the width of a small room, Sherrod again called to them, commanding that they let him go on ahead. This was his game, and when they saw the look in his eyes they remembered their promise and allowed him the required ten feet he wished to precede them.

A narrow trail followed, leading its winding way through a steep cañon, climbing gradually, then dropping swiftly. And in a little while they rode through a clump of trees, through a rude gate hidden by the trees and into the rock corrals.

And now a broad trail led unmistakably across the Bar Diamond, through the south pass there, and toward the broken country beyond. The fifty head of steers had gone that way, and not over a couple of hours ago. It was very plain.

"Think of it," muttered Hard Ross. "We had 'em so scared all the time that they had to keep them fifty head in that little valley! Lord, it must of took a powerful lot of hay!"

He seemed to find a certain satisfaction in that.

"I think our way is marked plain enough for us now," said Sherrod thoughtfully. "Plummer chased down here as soon as he knew that Dawn Madden would tell her story. He got his men busy; they put every hoof on the run. There was only one thing which Plummer could do then. He'd have the stock run back into the broken country, he'd have his men scatter them and leave them. It'll be a week's work for us bunching them and —"

"Look!" whispered Sunny Harper.

Farther down the valley, riding slowly toward the Bar Diamond bunkhouse, were seven men. Bull Plummer rode at their head.

"I thought so!" muttered Sherrod. "They've scattered the steers and have come back the roundabout way. And now what?"

"Now," spat out Mute Adams, who with Little John had come up with the others, and who remembered a horse with a broken leg, "it's just made 'em come acrost."

"Go easy there, Mute!" commanded Sherrod. "You take orders from me, understand? Don't you see that they are ready for trouble? Three of them are carrying rifles, every man of them is heeled. Why, man, it would take just about two minutes for a dozen saddles to be running empty! I don't want any wholesale murder this morning — if there is any other way," he muttered under his breath.

Plummer and his men had bunched a little. Plummer was now riding with a man on each side of him, and they were coming on more slowly, their eyes hidden yet by the distance. They were heading straight for the stable.

Sherrod measured the distance with his eyes; he saw that his party was a fraction nearer the Bar Diamond clutter of buildings. He formed his plan and shouted suddenly:

"Come on! Keep the barn between us and them! We get under cover first. Then we'll see what Plummer's got to say!"

He jammed his spurs home, leaned low in the saddle, and shot ahead toward the Bar Diamond corrals. His men, a few yards behind him, came racing after him, thinking that they saw his plan only a part of which they had guessed. In a body they reached the corral, the big barn standing between them and the clatter of Plummer's party. They drew rein, heard a curse from Plummer, knew that he, too, had stopped.

"What do you fellers want?" Plummer was shouting angrily. "I told you the next time you showed up on Bar Diamond property I'd chase you off."

Sherrod swung down from his saddle, left his horse with dragging reins, and stepped out from behind the barn.

"You boys keep under cover," he said coolly, his voice carrying distinctly to where Plummer was waiting. "This is just between Plummer and me. If Plummer's men keep out of it, let them go; it's just Plummer we want. If they are fools enough to cut in

208

you boys can pick them out of their saddles! Steady now, Mute! Not a shot until they start it. Then give 'em hell!"

He walked out into plain sight. Hard Ross groaned a little, took a step to follow, saw that every man of the Up and Down outfit was ready to forget his promise and go on after Sherrod, and then, his voice very hard, remembering that he was Jim Sherrod's foreman, he said sharply:

"Do what he says! He knows what he's doing. But, Sunny, you an' Happy get them rifles of your'n damn ready! Watch them two men on each side of Plummer. If they make a pass, you boys get 'em first!"

"Stop there, Sherrod!" Bull Plummer's voice, full of menace, was shaking with anger. "Stop or I'll drop you!"

Bull Plummer's gun was in his hand and rested upon the horn of his saddle, requiring to be raised only a few inches to bring the heavy muzzle in line with the advancing man. Jim Sherrod's guns were in their holsters, Jim Sherrod's hands were swinging, empty, at his sides. And still he came on with the same quick, even stride with which he had left the corral.

"You men," he shouted to Plummer's gang, "keep out of this! I don't want you! You can go — get out of the country for all I care and save your necks another year or so. Plummer," and the voice was as hard as the ring of steel on steel, the eyes stern and watchful, "you keep your gun down! I've got something to say to you."

"Say it, then!" boomed Plummer. "Say it quick, or I'll kill you!"

"You won't kill me," Sherrod told him coolly. "You'll never get the chance, and I think you know it. I knew that you were a thief all the time, Plummer; I think that you are a coward, too. Now sit still and listen: I want back every head of those fifty steers! I want you to take your men and drive them back into the Up and Down. I want that five hundred dollars I let you cheat me out of. I want seventy-five dollars a head for every cow that has been lost to the outfit for a year. Then I want you to get out of the country. Easy, there, Plummer." He had stopped, not twenty short paces from the man; he could see Plummer's eyes now. "I don't want to kill you!"

"You don't want to kill me!" snarled Plummer. "Why, you damned little dandy, I could —"

There came a sudden cry from one of Plummer's men, a man who had been at the rear and who now first saw Jim Sherrod very clearly.

"Hell!" he shouted. "It's the Painted Rock man! It's Fancy Jim Sherrod! Plummer, you fool, drop your gun!"

Fancy Jim Sherrod! Plummer's men were muttering the name among themselves. A hard smile came to Hard Ross's face.

"They know him now," he whispered. "They'll go powerful slow."

But into Plummer's eyes had flared a terrible rage.

"You damned little sneak!" he thundered.

The rest happened like lightning. The men at Plummer's right and left, as if electrified by the menace in Plummer's raucous voice, jerked their horses aside, their spur rowels sinking deep and sending their mounts leaping to right and left. Plummer's gun was jerked up. Plummer fired, the bullets pouring from his automatic almost in a steady stream of lead.

Jim Sherrod seemed to fall, and only an eye as quick as light could have told that he dropped to his knee and went sidewise just before instead of a second after the first shot. As he went down his right hand sped on its swift, grim, certain way to his hip; his gun was in his hand; he fired once; he was on his feet again; he fired again; he jammed his gun back in its holster before Plummer's heavy body, falling, had struck the ground.

It grew very still. Plummer's men did not move; with their guns hard in their hands, they waited for a shot from Sherrod's men. The Up and Down men were as motionless.

For a long moment after the echoes died down there was no sound save the creak of saddle leather, the jingle of bit-chains and spur-chains. And then the man who had warned Plummer that it was Fancy Jim Sherrod rode forward and threw his gun down.

"Plummer was a fool," he said colourlessly. "I told him to drop his gun." He shrugged his shoulders and felt for his tobacco. "What's the use a man just committing suicide that away, huh?"

"Plummer isn't dead!" said Jim Sherrod. "Pick him up, some of you men. Lay him in the shade by the corral there."

"You mean," gasped the man who had thrown down his gun, "that you missed? That close, two shots an' you didn't kill him? Say, you are Fancy Jim Sherrod an' I know it. Then what's happened to you?"

And of all the men who heard Fancy Jim Sherrod's quiet answer Hard Ross was the only one who fully understood.

"Maybe the light was in my eyes," he said coolly. "If he is alive now, he can thank the Dawn for it!"

CHAPTER
NINETEEN

Jim Sherrod had played his game his way and the fight was over. Just three shots from Bull Plummer, just two from Sherrod, and the men who had followed Plummer so long and who now saw him twisting in an agony of pain on the ground, were done with him. Plummer was not a man with a personality to call upon other men for warm friendship and loyalty; their relations had been purely relations of crooked business. Now the crooked business was at an end. Sherrod was willing to let them get out of the country; he wanted only his stock back, they wanted only to move on.

Slowly revolvers went back into their hidden places, rifles were laid over saddles, and two men, swinging down, lifted Bull Plummer and carried him to the shade along the corral fence. And they saw that the light had not been too bad for Sherrod's bullets to find right and left shoulder, and to put Plummer where his nerveless hands could no longer hold a revolver.

"There's just one thing, Jim," Hard Ross was saying, his eyes troubled. "While we're here —"

"Silver Slippers?" cut in Sherrod quickly. "I haven't forgotten her, Ross."

He turned to the two of Plummer's men standing at Plummer's side.

"Where is Ross's mare?" he asked point-blank.

"She's a devil!" grunted one man shortly. "What a man wants with the like of her —"

"She's the finest little mare ever put a clean foot on a dirty range!" flared up Hard Ross angrily.

The man shrugged his shoulders.

"Plummer was crazy about her," he retorted. "He always was crazy about a pretty horse, same as some men about a pretty woman. He made Hawley turn the trick an' paid him han'some for it. An' a lot of good it done Plummer, an' while he damn near killed her he never rode her more'n seven jumps at —"

"Plummer damn near killed Silver Slippers!"

Hard Ross's voice was suddenly so low that the man nearest him hardly heard it. Plummer, where he half sat, half lay against the corral, turned quick, widening eyes upon Ross, for Plummer had heard and he had understood the emotion making the low tones husky.

"Go look at her," laughed the man offering the information. "You'll find her hide pretty near cut to strips — not with a spur, seeing he couldn't stick on her long enough — but with a whip! An' when he was tired beating her an' she was all trembly in them thin legs of hers, she'd whirl an' try to beat his head off with her hoofs."

"Where is she?" snapped Hard Ross, his lean fingers sinking deep in the man's arm so that the fellow winced.

214

"I didn't touch the dirty outlaw," he snarled. "She's in the stable."

Ross flung him away and strode toward the stable, throwing the corral gate wide open and not tarrying to close it behind him. Sunny Harper, standing near the stable, opened the double doors. And Silver Slippers, her dainty silken hide cut with the merciless bullwhip which had worn deep into her delicate body and had never reached the unbroken spirit, flashed out into the corral, her eyes wide with terror and hatred, her nostrils distended, her fine ears pricked up, her proud head lifted high upon an arched neck.

"Silver Slippers!" cried Hard Ross, his voice breaking a little.

But she did not see him, she did not hear now the voice which she loved above all other sounds in the world. She saw the open corral gate, she scented liberty with her flaring nostrils, she flashed through. And as she went, like some glorious creature bred of the morning, all fire and life and leaping pride and tameless strength, she saw Bull Plummer against the corral fence — and she remembered.

Men leaped out of her way, someone crying shrilly!

"Look out! She's a man-killer!"

Plummer saw and settled a little to one side, trying to draw back, his eyes full of terror. But Silver Slippers struck, struck once, hard and mercilessly, with her forefeet, wheeled, shot out her hind hoofs unerringly. And more than one man, used to the things of a hard life, involuntarily covered his white face with his hands. Then Silver Slippers had gone, her racing blood leaping, speeding back home; and Bull Plummer had paid to the uttermost his long score.

The missing steers once more grazed on the Up and Down, the boys stood out at the corrals smoking and talking quietly, and Hard Ross in the stable, his eyes very tender, was putting liniment into the cuts upon Silver Slipper's shiny coat. The liniment burned, the tender flesh twitched under it, but Silver Slippers did not draw back from the man she trusted in all things. Her soft nose rubbed gently against Hard Ross's side, and her eyes, too, were tender.

At the bunkhouse door Fancy Jim Sherrod and Dawn had grown silent, as silent as the dusk creeping down through the valley. A moment ago and he had been speaking with a forced lightness, seeking to draw the girl's thoughts away from those last days of tragic happenings. To get her mind as far away as might be from Plummer and Madden and Hawley, he had spoken of the city.

"You'll be going back soon now," he had said.

And then it had been that he broke off and went to the door, staring out with darkening eyes, and the deep silence fell upon them.

Almost, in the bitterness of his thoughts, he had forgotten the girl herself who had inspired them; he was thinking of to-morrow and the days beyond it, and he sensed how empty they were going to be. But of a sudden she was at his side; at last she was speaking softly.

"Hard Ross has told me all that happened when you came up with Bull Plummer," she was saying and Sherrod turned to look down into her uplifted face. "I know why you didn't kill him. I know why you risked your life, just wounding a man when you might have shot him dead, a man who was even then seeking your death. For Ross told me what you said when you explained to them why you spared him!"

He turned his moody eyes back to the line of willows following the crooked wanderings of the valley creek.

"You should never have come in touch with a life like this, nor with a man like me," he said thoughtfully. "It is a hard life; it makes hard men. If in some little thing you can feel that I am not the brute you thought —"

"You are the kind of man this country needs!" she cried warmly. "To-day another man than you might have brought about the deaths of many men. You might have killed Plummer — justly! And you spared him. I have seen that you can be hard when there is the need. I have seen that you can be gentle, very gentle with a horse, with a wounded friend, with a woman —"

Now, suddenly, the moodiness was gone from Jim Sherrod's eyes before the brightness in Dawn's.

"Dawn!" he said quickly. "Dawn! Play fair with me, Dawn!"

"Play fair with you?" she asked, puzzled a little.

"I mean," he told her with a strange sort of fierce tenderness in his low-dropped voice, "that you mustn't look at me like that unless —"

"Unless?" she repeated after him, challengingly, her voice steady, her eyes steady upon his.

She lifted her head a little and held herself erect, her chin raised slightly, her deep grey eyes low-lidded and cool. And yet, despite the calmness of her attitude, slowly her face went crimson.

"I love you, Dawn. You know that, don't you?"

"And I love you. You didn't know, did you?"

Again were they silent. But now the silence was not like that that marks the coming of dusk, but rather that glorious still prelude to a golden daybreak.

"Say, Harpie," Happy Day was saying thoughtfully, "ever notice that look in Ross's eyes when he's alone with Silver Slippers and don't know anybody's looking at him? Just like a man with the only woman."

"Look up to the bunkhouse," Sunny Harper chuckled. "At Fancy Jim Sherrod! Don't it sorta remind you of the way Ross looks at Silver Slippers, huh?"

Well, after all, as Hard Ross had said:

"There is just one thing in the world as counts!"